AF508434

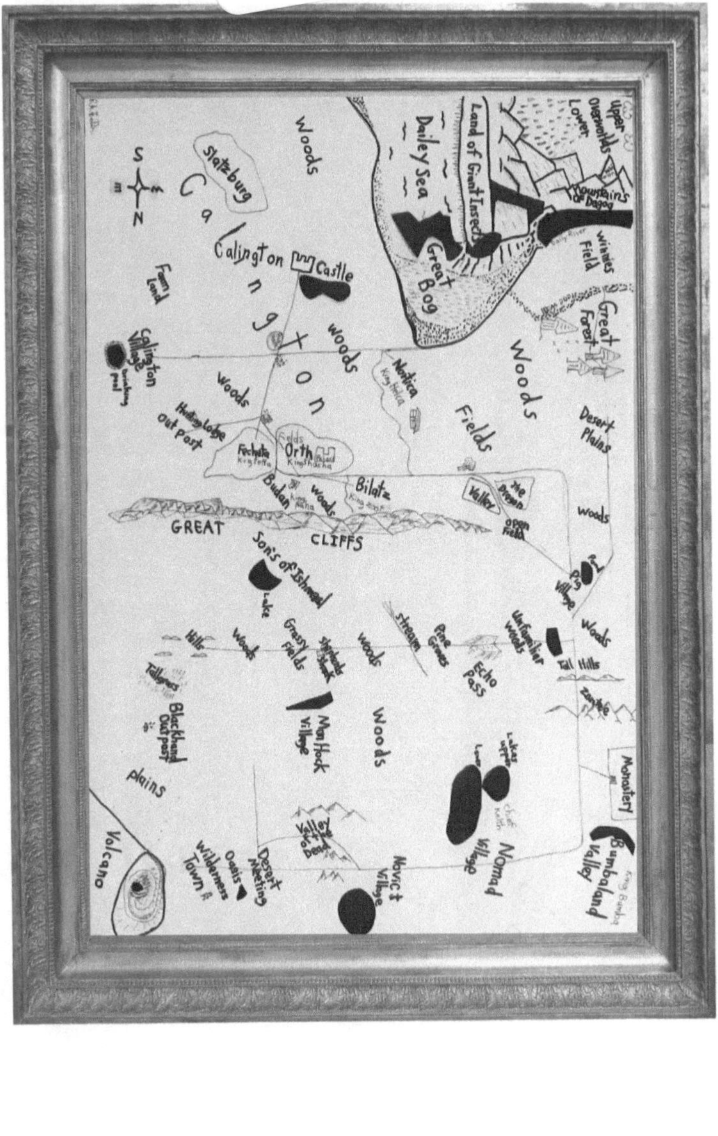

Upper
Overworlds
Lower
Mountains of Dagag
Land of Great Insed
Dailey Sea
Woods
Statzburg
Great Bog
Canixton
Calington Castle
Farm Land
Calington Village
Winnies Field
Great Forest
Woods
Desert Plains
Nortica Kingdom
woods
Fields
Hunterlodge Out Post
Fechita Kingdom
Orth Kingdom
Budan Kingdom
Bilata Kingdom
The Dream
Valley
open field
GREAT CLIFFS
woods
Village
Woods
Son's of Ishmeal
Lake
Hills
woods
Grassy Fields
Stream
Pine Groves
Unfamiliar woods
Tall Hills
Echo Pass
Talkpass
Blackhand Out Post
Man Hock Village
Woods
Lakes upper Lower
Chief lands
Monastery
Bumbaland Valley
King Bumba
Nomad Village
Plains
Valley of the Dead
Desert Meeting
Oasis
Wilderness Town
Novic Village
Volcano

# Calington Castle VII

## The Vision Revealed

R. A. Feller

ISBN 979-8-988-5027-9-1 (paperback)
ISBN 979-8-988-5027-8-4 (eBook)

Copyright: TXu 2-167-725
2/26/23



Printed in the United States of America

Edited

By

Jamison

This book is dedicated to those who want to
come out of darkness and enter into light.

# The Seducer

At a well in the center of the village near the monastery of Ostrog, a youth is out drawing water for his parents when a dwarf approaches him, "Well, what would your name be, young fella?"

"Olie."

"Olie, would you do an old man the kind service of fetching him a drink of water?"

"Would you be the old man?"

"Yes, I would."

Olie draws some water from the well. "Well, old man, what is your name so I may know who I am helping?"

The dwarf thanks him for his kindness as he takes the water.

Handing him a ladle from the bucket, Olie says, "Here you are."

The dwarf replies after taking a drink, "My name is Chaffie and as a reward, I would like to bless you for your service. Please receive my special stone." He takes out a green gem from his side pouch and holds it in his open hand.

"Wow! What a beauty. It is far beyond anything I've ever found or seen before. It is special."

"Even beyond this, it will show you favor in obtaining whatever you desire as long as you carry it."

"I don't know. I better check this out with my parents first."

"Yes, by all means as it is wise to honor them. Who knows? I may have stones for them, too. Perhaps even enough for the whole village, for your manners speak of everyone's character here."

"I will go and fetch my father from the fields after I finish my chores or I will never hear the end of it."

Olie quickly carries off his bucket of water as Chaffie slyly smiles and shouts after him, "I'll be here!"


At another location, a bell sounds at the Monastery to call the priests to ready themselves for a regiment of prayer. All file into the courtyard and stand attentively, awaiting instruction from the Monsignor. As Claude enters the yard last from ringing it, the Monsignor begins to share, "There will be a fasting rotation of eighths every three days. For those of you who have newly arrived, this means every three days, fifteen of you will fast for our traveling mercies and safe return while we are away. Brother Bartholomew will be in charge during my absence. So, you will all be able to focus more diligently on your prayers, I have just learned of a new evil in our lands which I must be going to Dagog to do battle against. These are all the details I know for now, but I will be learning more while on route by the visions Marcus has had. They will be further disclosed to me during travel.

So, without any further delay, will our instructors of the faith please raise your hands that Morris and Nettle may see them? Now as there are three of you, Thomas, you being the eldest in the lot, shall accompany us. There is a new village in our province not far from the mountains of Zantee. Gather your belongings and canteen, for you will be accompanying Sono, Marcus, and I as far as this village. For they are in need of a priest."

"Yes… Monsignor." Turning, the eldest goes for his belongings.

The Monsignor looks over and gives instruction, "Now for you two little ones, I do not know how long correspondence will take to reach our seat of The Great One's authority established here on earth. So, I recommend you two stay on and be trained in the faith to rightly divide the words from the *Book of Life.*"

Looking to one another, Morris and Nettle say at the same time, "I will do it!" They chuckle to themselves.

"You can put down your hands now, Manfried. You too, Gyus. Go to them now and be sure to pay close attention in your studies, for you shall be teaching others to contend for the faith as well."

Thomas returns winded and while catching his breath, our leader responds, "You didn't have to run. We would have waited."

I, Marcus, begin to chuckle, "You remind me of someone I once knew."

"Who would that be?"

"Why me, of course."

Sono looks on with an inquisitive smile of his own, "I wish I could have been there for your whole original Journey."

The Monsignor looks on, "We might be having just as interesting a journey this time, too."

Bartholomew interjects, "Quite right!"

Meanwhile, back at the village, Olie arrives with a large bucket of water. He sets it down on a table, picks up a broom, and begins sweeping the floor. His mother, Suma, enters the hut and suggests, "Olie, why don't you join your father in the fields? He'll be clearing more rocks today, so we might have additional land for planting vegetables. You can take him some roasted chicken with potatoes and do me the favor of a trip."

"Okay, ma." He starts for the door with basket in hand before remembering, "Hey ma, when I was getting some water this morning, there was a strange little man in town by the well. He offered me a little green stone that sparkled real nice for getting him some water while saying something about how the stone would show me favor in whatever I did for just being kind. He even said how he had gems for you and possibly the rest of the village. Can I have it?"

"You did good, Olie. I will check with the town elder and have an answer for you by the time you get back from the fields." A very excited Olie starts on his way.

The elder is checking the supply of grain in the storehouse when Suma walks up to him, "Trevor, I have been looking all over for you."

"What has you so uneasy, Suma?"

"There is a stranger in town who has offered Olie a special precious stone for the kindness of just drawing some water for him from out of our well."

"Was it mentioned why the stone is so special?"

"He was told it would show him favor for whatever he desired."

"Where is Olie supposed to meet the stranger?"

"He said at the well."

"I will have word sent to everyone in our village to meet outside the village for a gathering. Suma, if you'd be so kind as to go to the fields and inform the men there, I would be grateful. Tell them we shall meet at the three o'clock sun, for we must meet this stranger in unity this afternoon so as to not let him disrupt our having a single mind."

"I am troubled as well. I will go and tell all who are working the fields."

# The Vision Revealed

On the road while traveling through Ostrog, the Monsignor starts to inquire of just what was seen in my vision. "What exactly did you see in those seeing pools out in the woodlands?"

"You were much younger than you are now for a start. So, what I saw in the seeing pools must have been from your past."

"Know it now, Marcus, there are certain things that happened in my past which I could have handled better concerning my family. So, much confusion led me to want to find peace and give me understanding because of my prior decisions in this place. Perhaps you saw something from those days which I can interpret through my newer and much wiser eyes."

"If what was revealed to me will be of any help, I will be honored to share."

"Please do so."

"The first thing I saw in my vision was a fight taking place among the caverns: The light was dim in the caves, a fire roared at its center, and the smoke escaped through some cracks within the heights of its roof. There were five sisters and that's when I saw you in your younger days, perhaps in the mountains of Dagog."

"Yes-yes, what happened afterwards?"

Well, a mud fight took place between the youngest…"

"…that would have been Katrina."

"…and the oldest sister."

"…Claire."

I believe the youngest, Katrina, was trying to get the approval of her sisters by swallowing a lizard. You were changing one of the babes clothes while the other quietly slept."

The Monsignor stops walking and raises his arms "Lord, have mercy! They were such precious babes."

"How do you ever expect me to tell you the full vision if you keep interrupting?"

"I'm sorry. I will contain myself from any more of my emotional outbursts."

"As I was saying, soon after the mud fight started, her other sisters joined in with the eldest against Katrina. She left the cavern in a flurry of mud being flung at her.

Outside of the cave, when she went to wash dirt from her face while beholding her image in a puddle, she cried out and pounded the water with her fist and said, 'I would do anything to have more power than my sisters!' When the water settled, she saw a dark hooded figure looking over her shoulder in the reflection. She turned to see who was standing there but no one was seen 'til she looked back to the puddle again. The dark angel then spoke:

"What has you so uneasy, Katrina?"

"My sister's bullying because of my powers not being formed yet."

"Do not be uneasy, for thou hold the knife of sacrifice."

"I do not understand what good that doth me."

"Be quick to trust me and you shall have the power you seek, more powerful than all of your sisters combined."

"I rejoice in what you say!"

"Take the spelling knife and prick your finger and allow it to drip on my reflection in the water, then all power shall be thine within time."

When Katrina followed the dark angel's instructions, the sky turned dark and cracked with lightning 'til a prevailing wind suddenly whipped her image together with the angel's. The puddle was violently disturbed as Katrina fell on the ground. Once the puddle was blown dry, her eyes closed and she lay still for a time 'till the storm completely passed.

Next, when she opened her mouth from sleep, the dark angel's words came at first and spoke with her until its words entered her thoughts to speak on her own, "You have one more task to perform and then my powers will flow at my... Errr! Thy will."

"My sisters will belong to me is all I need to know. What is required?"

"Destroy the female babe and thou wilt be free to practice evil at will. Whatever thy desire shall be thine, stronger thy shall be than all of your sisters powers combined."

"I cannot do this as the babe is kin to my own bone."

The dark angel came out of her eye and whispered in her ear, "Thou hast seen thy sister abort many a babe for greater obligations many times. It wilt be like one of them. 'Tis one interests me. Know my word to be true in blood as it is not like others but special.

Doth pain of heart not be aching more than the reward of this babe's life? Do not let it get in your way as I promise there will be more!"

"So, this is how Katrina got her powers that day? This is how the sleep of doom was put on her. It is a good thing I stole the babe away with me that day. Now, Ashley has thrived to bless all in concern.

Thomas rejoices and joins in, "Yes, she has!"

"You two have broken my vision again. Let us walk 'til it returns."

"I have faith it shall return. Are we walking too fast for you, Sono?"

"Being a dwarf, my feet have learned to be quick."

Back at the new village in Ostrog, a meeting is taking place concerning the stranger at the well. Out of sight from Chaffie's view, the people are listening to Trevor gather more information from Olie about the dwarf."

"You are not in any trouble, Olie. I just want to go over your conversation with Chaffie, that is all."

"Well, there is not much to tell. He told me about how the stone could get me whatever I wanted and when I suggested how I should ask permission, he said, "It is wise to honor your parents.""

"Anything else at all?"

"Now that you mention it, he said he may have enough for us all because I was raised so proper."

Someone shares their voice on the matter, "It sounds like he is familiar with our customs, maybe he is not bad after all."

Trevor responds by saying, "Perhaps that is what he wants us to believe. Gem charms are not a part of our traditions and if we started to rely on them, would it not distract us from better knowing The Great One?"

Another voice speaks out, "Why not let the boy have it and see if it has any effect on him? Then we would know if the stranger is okay or not. Are you not putting the boy to the test for your own personal gain, which would remove you from having the unity of knowing that Godliness with contentment is great gain? If anything should happen to Olie, would this not break our unity as well? Shall what is evil not try to divide a people, setting them at odds with each other? When are we supposed to love one another in Spirit and in truth in this case?

I believe now would be the time to remind you that we have agreed to wait for a teacher to come from the monastery to establish us in full unity."

Suma steps forward and stands next to Trevor while speaking up as well, "Can we really receive what this stranger has to offer without question? We do not yet have full understanding of covenant with The Great One of truth. So, how will we truly measure any counsel when we have nothing to compare it with to see whether it be true?"

Someone else calls out, "I say we show the stranger some hospitality and when the priests show up, hear them both in what they have to say, then we will have a choice."

Trevor nods his head before speaking, "This seems to be a good idea, but we must pray first to remain in unity. So, we all shall be in complete agreement to see if peace within the village will remain while before the stranger. We should all be at rest to know if he will try to disrupt our unity or not."

Someone who has come from the field says, "I agree. Now let us get on with the rest of the day."

"In your mind you agree, but not fully within your impatient heart. For I said that we will pray 'til we had peace in unity. Your attitude is not of peace and gratitude, but places yourself ahead of God."

"You are right. I will pray with patience until we have unity again."

# The Meeting

The sun hangs around four o'clock in the afternoon sky as we approach the village. The Monsignor is confirming what was told to him by Marcus. "So, according to your other vision, this Chaffie fellow has undergone the same sleep of doom, too. Him being, Katrina's apprentice sounds serious."

"How so?" Thomas inquires.

"Because Chaffie was Katrina's apprentice, they would have had a common bond. When she lost her powers, they could have entered into him, making him twice as dangerous."

Marcus reminds, "It is a good thing The Great One protects us or we would have been done in by Chaffie while in the wagon with us before."

Sono becomes involved, "I hope the Lord will continue to deliver us as I have no desire to be under any spell by stone or any other means again."

Chaffie raises his head from a slumber while sitting on the ground and leaning against a wall at the well. He notices our dust being kicked up on the road and sees us on the approach.

When we arrive at the village, the streets are empty. Concern turns to faith within our minds as we watch all the villagers come out to meet us at the well.

"What a pleasant surprise! Thank you for such a wonderful greeting."

Trevor inquires of us, "We are glad you are pleased, Marcus, but was no one else here when you arrived?"

"No. Were you expecting someone else?"

"This is Olie. Perhaps you remember him from your last visit. He will fill you in on the details of who he met here earlier today."

"Hi, Olie. While we are at it, let me make some other introductions. This is our Monsignor from the monastery. Sono, you already know, and last but not least, this is Thomas who will be remaining with you. He is a teacher priest that shall make sure you will practice your faith with full understanding to prevent any darkness from creeping in."

The Monsignor gets involved, "Thank you, Marcus, you have given us a fine introduction. Thomas will be instructing you on how all of creation is interlocked in cycles. Knowing their importance will reveal to you how water baptism ties in with the reception of the Holy Eucharist. All shall come into focus. You shall be prepared to understand how there is a co-mingling of the Holy Spirit moving upon water within the substance of His living word. It will further be revealed how we as His bride await the true essence of Himself while anticipating her bridegroom. You will soon be able to join us in our heavenly feast at the thanksgiving meal of sacrifice with an understanding that will satisfy you.

Thomas becomes involved, "Yes! When you are baptized in the name of the Father, Son, and Holy Spirit, you co-mingle with the word by being immersed to become one with water through the creation of God's word, which makes you His bride and a part of the church."

The Monsignor looks over at the well, "Then you will learn when you are one with water as The Great One's bride. You will be ready to be impregnated with life through Holy seed by resurrection found in His presence of Eucharist, the bridegroom himself. You will receive eternal life from this re-creation in the oneness of being in unity with water which evaporates and ascends into the co-mingling of everything in the atmosphere. For when completion enters into the incomplete, transformation takes place from within.

Now, just as water goes through the firmament and ascends into heaven, so do we. Passing through the door of our earthen flesh, we co-mingle with the Eucharistic seed of the groom and experience eternal life by resurrection power. We enter through the door of God's friction, heat, fire, and light by slowing down. Through this gate, evaporation takes place. Our fleshly desires decrease here line upon line, here a little there a little, one precept at a time as God increases inside."

A very pregnant villager passes by and catches all eyes.

"It will all take place within the essence of our beings within our living souls through the womb of water baptism. Once unified through this act, everyone will co-mingle with all the elements found in our earthen flesh to receive seed through the Holy Eucharist, our male groom and Christ, for a full re-creation to take place.

I have given you an overview of everything you will be learning from Thomas. Now, should evil try to seduce you into wanting more than what you actually need or cause you to seek out comforts to blot out your memories of how you are loved by The Great One, you have been informed. For when unhappy, you must always be reminded of the value you possess by knowing the eternal life He has conceived within. He will always bring joy by meeting every need when drawing near. This is how we grow into being eternally alive and seated in heavenly places with Him.

Trevor gets excited, "I look forward to learning more of what will be taught us, but there is a matter which presses upon my mind from the last things you have spoken."

"What would that be?"

"I was going to have Olie tell you about the strange dwarf who was at the well before you arrived, but after all that was said about being distracted from God meeting our needs with His love, I must make mention that he did try to break up our unity by offering us special stones, which were to show us favor in whatever we desired."

I interjected, "Did he say what his name was?"

Olie replies, "Chaffie."

"The nature of creation cries out against strange charms as they go against the nature of truth itself by the seduction of created things in place of The Creator. Only The Great One is to be worshiped. So, do not admire the craft of man over the creator's hand who fashions everything on any level at all. For if you become distracted by craft replacing creation, you will miss what truly sparkles in the glory of God's light.

The Monsignor, Sono, and I look to one another. Sono speaks up, "Trevor, I have been quiet until now and have done a lot of listening as have you all. Sometimes I do not hear so good. So, according to what has just been said, "Do you believe Chaffie to be a friend that would draw one closer or would he draw one further from the Great One?"

"His actions were to flee when he saw you coming and he did not originally come in the character of The Great One"'s name but according to his own."

"This being the case, do you have a place where we could talk out of the wind? For I have a private matter to discuss with you."

How come we cannot talk here?"

"I will explain once we are inside."

"Very well."

Trevor leads the way as we follow right behind. We step inside a nearby hut across from the well. The Monsignor questions, "Is there another way that you know for us to leave your village beside the pass through the mountains of Zantee?"

"Why did we have to come in here for you to ask me this?"

"There are spirits which ride upon the wind that can carry words of conversation to those who know how to use these winds. We suspect Chaffie knows how to do this."

"I understand now. Though, we did not come from the mountain pass of Zantee when we first settled here."

"Where did you come from?"

"Well, it has been awhile now. So, it might be safe to return."

"Return from where?"

"There is a path that we cut out alongside the mountain sides of Zantee as known by you. West of them leads to the ocean. We were originally fishermen until a strange sickness came. Many of us died, so we fled here."

"How long has it been since you left the ocean?"

"About 80 moons ago."

"That is pretty close to seven years," says Sono.

"I have studied situations like this in the past and say it is worth the risk."

The Monsignor further inquires, "Are there any boats there?"

"Yes, but they have not been maintained unless some of our people survived the sickness which remained behind."

"Do you have a place where Thomas can stay?"

"He can stay in the storehouse until we build him a hut."

"Is there any way you can show us where the path begins to the ocean?"

Olie can take you there. He knows the way to this path."

"Why not stay the night and start out in the morning?"

"It will be dark soon and having a long journey, we must set out."

"I will call for Olie while you bid your farewells."

The four of us join hands and pray as Sono leads us, "Lord, we stand before you as travelers. Keep us safe in the unknown lands we go to."

Thomas shares his concerns, "Great One, give me the wisdom I need to proclaim your faith. Always keep me true to you and grant my brothers success on their mission."

The Monsignor speaks his mind, "Bring presence of mind to my sisters when we have council with them on how to do away with the lower realm. Guide us on how to close this door on evil without any doubts.

I close by sharing my heart, "Be a father to us and protect all of your children. Teach us how to know You better during our travels. Amen."

Trevor returns with Olie who is briefed on showing us the path. We leave at once.

# Unexplored Territory

At first, we are led off in the direction of the tall cornfields. Upon entering them deep enough, we manage to turn and slip out the side and go over a hill in the gray of dusk. Olie leads us on.

The Monsignor shares what is on his heart, "You are very brave, Olie. On the way back, if you encounter your friend you met at the well earlier, run. For his mind is cunning and his thoughts are continually evil."

"I know how to handle him."

Perhaps it would be better if you remained in the cornfields until morning…"

"…but we are…"

I am quick to cover his mouth with my hand and make a gesture about the wind. Olie nods his head in response. We move on silently 'til we come to an opening in some thickets which lead to tall trees and an open path. There has been a lot of overgrowth from years of lack of use. Olie waves us on and we make it through okay. The moon shines, breaking through the darkness of the trees. We start on our way.

Olie makes it back to the cornfields and begins to cover the tracks from the direction of our departure 'til he is past where we made the turn to leave the field. He now starts to make his way back out of the cornfields from where we first entered in. All at once, he is pushed to the ground by Chaffie who seemed to be waiting for him by the opening. He brandishes a rock over him and shouts, "Where are those priests?" Olie springs to his feet and begins to run as the rock sings past his ear. Chaffie whistles loudly and a pack of wild dogs are heard barking off in the distance as Chaffie smiles.

Sono steps out in front of us and takes the lead, saying, "You two had better follow me as I can see the path better."

"I guess being short comes in handy for some-thing after all."

"I heard that, Marcus!"

"I only jest because you are not the only one around here who was designed specially." I proudly display my hand as he responds.

"Ha, ha! Come on, let's continue. Seeing in these moon shadows is hard enough without any dark words. You two better watch for branches as the trail up ahead is not easy."

"Wait a minute!" We stop… and going into my pack, I pull a long knife from out of its sheath. "This shall do nicely."

Sono volunteers, "You better lead now, Marcus. I do not want to know of any accidents."

I step out in front and begin to notch and cut my way through the moonlit forest. "Monsignor, as you were saying before, about those of us who believe the door to evil can be closed, what will it take?"

"Growing pains, which shall cause us to lose our life for The Great One so we might gain what leads to greater contentment, will surely be a part of the solution."

Looking at the difficulty of making cuts in the shadowy branches causes me to share my thought, "I wonder if there be a clue here in the closing of this door within the cuts of the shadows that I make."

Sono becomes involved, "I do not believe you two should be talking. I remember something about voices being carried in the wind."

I respond by saying, "You forget. We are under the cover of trees which break the wind, along with the leaves which have fallen upon the ground and silence our sounds."

"I guess I was overstepping my bounds."

"We are all learning."

The Monsignor rejoins the conversation, "Speaking of learning, what were you talking about before, Marcus, when you said how cutting in the dark was as a clue to closing the door upon evil? What were you seeing?"

"What if evil was keeping everything dark so we could not find the embrace of God's love? Could we not reason that separation from it causes us to thirst for The Great One's bond of a full embrace? After all, doth verse from *The Book of Life* not say, 'If you search for Me with all your heart you will find me?'"

Sono asks, "Monsignor, if what Marcus is reasoning is accurate, could the verse, 'Walk in the light while you have the light that darkness doth not overtake you,' from the *Book* be reasoned to mean we do not just walk in the light but always towards the light?"

"Now you are starting to understand the mercy of grace as it allows us to wander off the path of light and return to it again 'til it is realized it is better than anything else."

"To add to what the Monsignor has said, 'Every gem has its setting and when we recognize darkness to be the poorer choice, we step into the light to remain.' For we are the crown of God's creation and sparkle brighter than any gem we could possess when truly set in our proper positions."

"Now I see what Chaffie was offering me was pale in comparison to the eternal life which The Great One wanted to place within me. I cannot believe that this fellow dwarf wanted to tarnish me from the sparkle of life and not enhance it by using charmstones to suit his own purposes. He led me to believe that I was in control while in time to remain in a fallen state of being all along. What purpose could he have possibly had in keeping me inside the darkness of time?"

I continue hacking away at the branches as I share my conclusion, "Those gemstones must lead to a center of power to drain lives and transfer them to his own. There must be a connection which stores up power while his victims become drained in the dimness of dark inside their mind. For while ever learning and never coming to the knowledge of the truth, a possessed essence of being must feed the power of the one who rules over them all. The one who rules the stones by the power they possess must cause them to blindly strive to survive while the owner collects his prize."

"I believe you're on to something, Marcus. For if the struggle to achieve success leads to raging against each other from a desire sparked forth to want more, then we'll strive not towards deeper love in time but a trap set to imprison us. It suits evil's purposes to keep man away from the embrace of deliverance in God's loving arms. For when He satisfies, contentment sets in to break all other bonds to pieces."

Sono shouts out, "Things done in rage makes us slaves and in love, kings!"

The Monsignor responds, "That was quite an insight on both your parts."

I suddenly break through into a clearing where the ground starts to slope upward and the trees are more spread out. The higher we climb, the brighter the moonlight starts to become as the clouds disperse. Further understanding this opens a gate within my mind. "Monsignor, I have observed something further since the shadow of the thickets."

"What has our Great One revealed that has you so excited?"

"There is a gradual climb out of darkness. It was confirmed on our advance towards the mountains as our steps have embraced more light on its slope. If the door to light is opened in varying degrees of light to brighten the mind, then perhaps the door to evil will close if we mature enough to remain within it."

My traveling companions say at the same time, "Thank God for His mercy!"

We come across some more overgrowth as I raise my long knife. "Thank God for His mercy indeed." I cut another narrow branch from a tree which grants us further passage.

Thomas stands before the lifeless body of Olie and asks, "How did this happen?"

"We found him in the field on our way to the gardens. Wild dogs are suspected of doing this."

"No. What I mean is, you may ask yourselves why did this happen when he served in the name of The Great One. So, why did he let this happen?"

Suma looks to Thomas through her husband's arms which hold her and asks, "Why?"

"I am sorry for your loss, Suma."

"Why should we serve a God who cannot protect his own?"

"The Great One doth protect his own and your son though he be dead is yet still alive because of it. This might be hard to understand, but God has granted Olie eternal life which he received before his body was destroyed. His promise to give him life as the giver of life has not changed. For in knowing the danger beyond doing the right thing, we introduced him to The Great One as the giver of eternal life before going out on mission with us. For any who are interested in learning with me about how faith in the Spirit behind The Great One's word became flesh, I have knowledge of how His essence dwells among us. Remember, I initially came to explain how *The Book of Life* sparks forth changes by the new covenant into eternal life which I would be willing to share at the appropriate time."

"Suma, who is listening to Thomas' words, says, "When the time is right, I will come." Many others nod in agreement as well.

While making my cuts in the forest, I notice the scent of the air to change. Soon after, the forest comes to an end while we embrace the full light of day. The waves of the ocean are seen on the horizon. Looking down the final slope of the mountain turned to hill country, we see a weathered town from off in the distance, which we start making our way to.

# The Abandoned Sea Port

Unknowingly, eyes are watching us enter the town and follow our every move while we walk the streets. Upon arrival, a breeze is felt from the ocean which alerts us to the possibility of our voices being carried to Chaffie.

The Monsignor places one of his hands on my shoulder and with the other motions to a faded storefront that we advance to. Sono tags along behind us 'til we are all inside and out of the wind. Sono volunteers, "I do not like it. There was supposed to be a plague here and yet there is not one dead body on the ground."

"You have a point, Sono. Monsignor, what do you say?"

"Wild animals or perhaps we haven't come across the bodies yet…"

"…Wait a minute! Did Trevor not tell us that all did not leave before? Maybe there are some here who are still alive."

Sono questions, "Then how come they did not greet us?"

The Monsignor makes a suggestion after seeing my knife yet in hand, "Your long blade could be taken as a weapon and a hostile act."

Well, if that be the case, shouldn't he keep it out to deter any from attacking us?"

I remove my pack from off of my shoulders and take out my sheath. I return it before placing it back in my pack.

Sono interjects, "We'll be defenseless without having that knife handy."

"How did we get here?"

"We walked!"

"So there will be no misunderstanding, God is watching over us. If I was to have my knife out as a weapon, it would break trust with The Great One because my faith would be in my knife. Make no mistake, our God is jealous over us. If we take matters into our own hands, we become a god unto ourselves in His eyes. So, unless directed by His voice from a position of peace, the knife stays in its sheath to honor Him. Now, I suggest you agree with us if you want to be under His protection, too."

"I agree."

The Monsignor smiles and says, "Bartholomew has trained you well."

"I only wish I could have been a better student."

"With that kind of attitude, I would be glad to pick up where he left off."

"I thought you already had?"

"What are you two talking about?

"How I am going to be training Marcus as his new mentor."

"Aren't you all the same?"

"No, we are all set under authority, which keeps us in a welcome place of humility."

"Are you saying that the one at the top has all the answers?"

"No-no! He sits in the judgment seat under The Great One's Spirit of authority to make sure all is in agreement with the character of Christ within the church."

How can he sit in judgment of you from all the way over here?"

"Consider this: as a mother hen sits over her brood of chicks and cares and trains them, so doth our leader who trains us to watch over The Great One's church. A mother hen doth not have to watch over her chicks in the same way. For as her love stays to continue to inform them of when her affirmations are not present, they have sight to see that without love there is danger."

I see. Since they are bound by love, this keeps the church together even though he is not present at all times. I have one more question."

"I thought you would. What would it be?"

"Who looks after your leader?"

"A new eternal mother of earth who is mother to him looks after us all as well. For not being part of a corrupted soil within a living soul that dies due to impurities like the first man, Adam, she becomes the first to bear a seed that regenerates within an original eternal and uncorrupted soil. We are now formed and filled within the new nature of this soil of graces in an eternal sense from before the fall of man by her faithfulness to God."

Sono sits staring attentively as he takes in all of what is being said.

"Now once being impregnated in the essence of water baptism as bride, we can meet with the bridegroom by this Holy Eucharistic seed because of her uncorrupted soil. We, too, through The Great One's new seed, take on an eternal nature of being faithful to God through His power initiated by The Great One's mother who has been faithful. He now shares with us His resurrection as co-heirs to His throne by the co-mingling craft of His Holy Spirit like a bee, which tickles a flower in the order of bearing fruit by the order of faithfulness. For *The Book of Life* states, "God is a rewarder of those who diligently seek Him."

My new mentor asks, "Well, Sono, do you have any further questions?"

Sitting down on the ground, he says, "I need a moment."

"That is not a bad idea. I suggest we all get some rest so we may refresh ourselves."

The Monsignor becomes concerned, "I am troubled in my spirit and need to pray about our first impression of entering this town with a drawn knife."

Sono speaks up, "Mind if I join you?"

I step up as well and joining hands, the three of us pray for wisdom. We join in agreement as my mentor speaks out, "Oh Great One, forgive my shortsightedness in allowing Marcus to enter into town with his blade unsheathed. What must we do to not appear to be a menace to this town?"

We wait in silence 'til our peace is restored. The Monsignor has a thought come to him, which evokes a response, "I have received a plan."

Leaving a small package of wrapped salted pork out from our supplies, a meal is left out as a peace offering on a nearby counter by the entranceway. We then doze off on our packs and begin taking in some much needed rest. While closing our eyes, the offering fades from our sight.

Waking to long shadows, we stretch ourselves back into existence. Sono notices, "Hey, the pork has been taken!"

I make mention, "Well, now we know we are not alone."

Sono speaks up again, "How do you know a wild animal didn't take it?"

My mentor suggests, "An animal would have shredded the wrapping and left some sort of sign before dragging it off. Would this not be the case?"

"You do have a point," says Sono.

"We now have to figure out whether our visitor be friend or foe."

The Monsignor looks at us and says, "I say friend, for we did not get our throats cut while we slept.

"Or, at least not yet," Sono suggests.

Hey, you smell something burning?"

"It seems like someone is inviting us to dinner."

"I believe you're right, Monsignor."

"Well, I guess they be friend because no one's gonna invite you to dinner if they were gonna cut your throat."

All of us look to one another before I ask, "Should we leave our packs?"

"Not me," says Sono.

"I am afraid I'm in agreement with Sono on this one. For would it not be a little premature on our part as of yet?"

I guess you two are right. We still do not know about the inhabitants of this town."

Sono comments, "It doth smell a little fishy at that."

"I believe that's dinner you're smelling, Sono. Come on, you two, I suggest you follow my example. Let's get packing and go see who's cooking."

Making our way to the seaport, we notice all the sea vessels in the water at the docks without crew while following the smokey scent from the fish fry, which is noticed at the end of the dock.

Sono is first to speak up again, "It has to be a trap!"

I advance, "Would anyone care to join me for dinner?"

"Sono, can't you see our favor is being returned for the meal we left out earlier by whoever this is?"

"I still say it's a trap, Monsignor."

"Suit yourself." My mentor follows along behind me.

"It could even be Chaffie!" Sono looks back at the empty seaport and town before realizing how alone he is. "Oh, wait for me. I am coming, too." He hurriedly takes off after them.

Upon arriving at the end of the dock, we discover a large kettle to rest on for large stones with a fire within it. Across its top lies an open lid with many narrow bars. On top of this lay several big fish on sticks and a large pan filled with roasted potatoes.

A voice is heard calling from the ocean on a mid-sized sailboat, "Ship ahoy!"

"Cantik is my name. Now, what brings two priests and a dwarf to the seaport of Cedwick from out of the mountains?"

"I am the Monsignor from the monastery at Ostrog. I see from the caution you use in the way that you have met us, Cantik, and the fact we woke to the smell of your good cooking that you be friend."

"I was not sure about you three at first either. For in seeing that long knife your partner carries there, I was not sure if you were hostile. Yet after leaving your salted pork out, I knew you could not be bad."

I am first to respond, "My name is Marcus and our short friend here be Sono."

"Well, I guess it's time you met my crew."

"Crew?" shouts Sono.

"Surely you did not believe that all the fish was just for the four of us."

The Monsignor smiles with a gesture, "I should have known better."

"You can come up now, gents." Cantik introduces them as they appear from below deck. "This be Skip, my first mate." He comes up from out of the hold at the bow with a slight nod. Cantik calls out, "Oxer!" He then comes out from the cabin at the stern and nods as well. "Do not let the size of my second mate trouble you as he is as gentle as lamb. Raise anchor and let's go in."

# The Strangers in Town

Standing on the dock, each of us enjoys a fish on a stick that eats tender, having been scaled, gutted, and cleaned. The pan is set to cool on a nearby prepstone set up as a table and we soon compliment the meal with a potato, which we wash down with water from our skins. Cantik and his mates wash down their food with tankards filled from a cask of ale.

Cantik's tongue becomes loosened by the ale and he starts to become a little overly friendly. "Say, why don't you priests join us in a little festive ale?"

My mentor responds, "I find life to be joyous enough for me already as I have a thirst for something a little more satisfying for me."

"Hey, wait a minute. Did The Great One Himself not turn water into wine at a wedding feast?"

"Yes, but in doing so, he puts out the old covenant to usher in the sign of the new. You know you cannot put new wine into old wineskins lest you burst the old one and all becomes lost. This is why The Great One must put new wine into new covenant vessels He has placed within you. Wherefore, after refashioning the essence of your being with this new covenant, you are becoming established within eternal life. For being consecrated by Him from within, you are now newly birthed inside."

Cantik sobers up upon hearing from the Monsignor. "That's not what I was originally taught. I thought you do not get eternal life 'til after you die but have salvation in the meantime while you await it."

"Have you not heard 'I must decrease that The Great One will increase?' Where do you go when decreasing while He increases all the more?"

Cantik's mates pour out their tankards of ale and sober up to listen as well.

The Monsignor continues, "How doth the dead in Christ rise again in resurrection without already having eternal life?"

Skip shouts, "No, soon we are going to see the king and not now! For we are not perfected yet to stand before a holy God."

I become involved, "Are we not to be anxious for nothing and walk with a peace which surpasses all understanding to guard our hearts and minds? Doth this not make us in the world and no longer of it?"

Oxer, who is a little bit slow in his speech, speaks up as well, "I have often wondered why my peace comes and goes so often."

The Monsignor speaks up again, "If you build on a firm foundation, then you truly know eternal life as it has no variable waves of motion in it. For when you take the time to build line upon line while looking at the plumb line, The Great One Himself, then you will not sink upon a foundation, which lacks the firmness of stability and become anxious again.

Make no mistake. We are to be established by eternal life in a heavenly realm while here on the earth. There is no placing flesh within the Spirit as they are at war with one another until the seed of the bridegroom protects His bride, which is the church.

For by co-mingling within it in deep affections, more so than anything else, it becomes pregnant with new life. This is where we are truly joined by Him to do all things which strengthens us."

Cantik questions, "How did you find us to bring such news in the first place?"

Sono shares his views on the matter, "We did not exactly know for sure anyone would be here."

Skip becomes intrusive, "Then why did you come?"

Cantik holds up his hand and quiets his first mate, "Now, let us be more courteous with our guests. You must forgive my first mate, we have not had company in a very long time, especially such refined gentlemen as yourselves."

The Monsignor speaks a kind word, "Skip asks a fair question and knowing you have not had company for awhile, it is sometimes hard to readjust."

A curious Cantik inquires further, "Well, how did you find out about the seaport here?"

"We were told that a seaworthy vessel might be found here."

"Who told you of Sedwick… and for what purpose would you need a craft?"

"A man who goes by the name of Trevor was discovered as the village leader of a settlement in Ostrog while en route to Dagog. We were told that your seaport was an alternative route."

"Trevor would not have disclosed our location unless there was a dire need on your part. What could be of such an urgent matter that you would risk plague, let alone try and manage a vessel as you three have the look of a bunch of landlubbers, not old sea dogs like us?"

"How did you know we knew about the plague?"

"Old Trevor has too caring of a heart not to warn you. I'm glad he's okay. He was smart to leave with the others when he saw the first signs. Now, what was so urgent that you came here?"

"We cannot talk out in the open as a sudden breeze can carry a voice anywhere. It would be best if we went into your cabin and discussed the matter there."

"The traveler who met with us at sea told us about voices carried in the wind, but we never paid him much mind 'til you just reminded us of it. Come on board the *Hope it Floats* as I am eager to hear why you've come."

Passing the forward cabins below deck and past the galley, we step inside the cabin at the end of the craft. Oxer is the last one in and as he closes the door behind him, we enter into the world of a rather spacious room having four bunks, a table with star charts, and two large benches which are mounted to the floor on either side. It is here we sit before a table in the midst of some fine carpentry with a thick coat of varnish on the wood which causes the grain to make itself known. After becoming accustomed to our surroundings to a setting sun, four oil lanterns are lit on beams that support the cabin. Once lit, Skip dims them down. He then joins us in sitting down next to Cantik who sits directly across from The Monsignor at the center of the table opposite of me. Oxer is near the door and Sono is across from him.

The three lean towards my mentor who starts to tell them of our mission, "I do not yet know how or even if it can be done, but I know there is an open realm of evil which needs to be closed."

"I can see why you've brought us inside to tell us."

"Cantik, if you would be good enough to pick us out a humble craft that we could manage, I would be forever in your debt."

"How about the longboat tied to our deck?"

"I was hoping for something with a sail."

"How about the larger boat it is connected to?"

I shout out, "You mean you would come with us?"

"From what the traveler, we met at sea has told about The Great One's character, it would now be a task worthy of our humble selves."

The Monsignor addresses Cantik and his men, "There are many dark perils which would not be safe for you."

Skip exclaims, "More so than being raised from the fires of hell when I was dead?"

"As was I when the traveler discovered me," says Oxer.

"Cantik, I take it you were alive to get the traveler's attention?"

"Barely."

"Did the traveler happen to mention his name?"

"He said it was more important that we remembered the name of The Great One. Then he set sail from our ship while at sea, after instructing us in the ways of salvation."

"Did he have a crew with him?"

"He did not permit us to board his ship, so I do not know."

"It is known that The Great One doth work all things for good for those who love Him. Yet it is known that His truth has a mercy that triumphs over judgment, too."

Cantik further inquires, "What is meant by mercy triumphs over judgment?"

"It means that we are all in different stages of growth and God is faithful to meet us in each one of them."

"You seem to know more than what we know as you have mentioned receiving eternal life while here on earth."

"Do you have parchment, quill, and ink for keeping a ship's log?

"I'll do better than that."

"Skip, would you be a good first mate and bring me my captain's book?"

Skip excitedly jumps up and retrieves it from a cupboard built into the walls of the cabin. Oxer is up as well and hands over the captain's quill and ink from the opposite side of the table.

"If it is your desire, you shall learn all we know tonight. For in understanding the experiences of our previous adventures, you will be ready to set sail with us on the morrow."

The three say together, "It is time, we be ready!"

# The Storm at Sea

At morn, we hoist anchor in The Great One's timing. Being up all night has not even phased us. Having received the seed of eternal life from the bridegroom for the first time, Cantik, Skip, and Oxer are truly rooted and grounded in The Great One's love as His bride. I admire the pink color of the sky as we set sail, leaving the port behind us before stepping back inside the cabin.

Cantik shouts to us from the wheel, "I shall have you there in possibly a day or two if all goes well. Skip, take the wheel. I have a story to deliver to The Monsignor and his traveling companions as promised. Keep me posted on any sudden weather changes, I will be in my cabin."

"Aye-aye, captain."

Looking out of a window flap held open by a stick from the stern of the ship, I watch the sun change position as we veer south from traveling west. Noticing how Skip masterfully has maneuvered the craft, it leaves me feeling at ease. The coast next comes into view from a window on the port side of the ship and we begin to sail the coast. I hear a creaking sound which diverts my attention. The door to the cabin opens and Cantik walks in.

"I believe we have a meeting, gents."

We sit at the table to the rocking of the waves as the bow cuts through the water rising and falling on its nose. Once settled, we become attentive to listen to what Cantik has to say.

The Monsignor now sits across from him with me to his right and Sono on his left not far from the door. Leaning towards us, Cantik begins to tell his story, "A very sad state of affairs has happened here at Cedwick. For we once were a thriving town, a bustling community with an active seaport. Or perhaps a little too active as it all seemed to unfold down at the seaport first. A ship arrived in tow infested with rats and half eaten remains of what was left of its dead crew. It should have been burned at once, but the greedy pirate merchants threatened to burn our town when an inspector seized a torch in hand to bring the ghost ship to an end after sizing up the situation.

Their greed blinded them to their own demise, which eventually led to the destruction of our whole community. By the time word reached Elderman Trevor, people began to drop at the port. The last thing I remember was setting sail to escape the mysterious plague before being roused at sea by the man of faith who told us about The Great One.

Upon returning to Sedwick, the sickness no longer had an effect on us after returning to the community." Moved with emotion, he folds over on the table with his head down weeping, "Everyone, all of our friends are dead! Until we heard news of Trevor from you, the rest we either burned or buried. Here we three have lived these past seven years hoping that others would return to us or at least visit our port, but no one has come 'til you."

The captain breaks down and begins to sob as my mentor extends his hand and places it on his arm to steady him. There-there now. It is better if you cry so that your healing can begin."

"Clang! Clang! A bell is heard followed by the voice of Skip, his first mate, "Captain, there is a storm approaching!"

I watch as Cantik's strength returns. Immediately, he takes action and shouts, "Oxer, away the anchor! Skip, drop the mainsail and prepare to batten down the hatches!" As he heads for the door, Sono shouts behind him, "Go for it, man!"

An incoming wind starts to violently rock the boat. A swell suddenly splashes at the starboard window. While standing in a puddle of water, the Monsignor is slammed against the side of the cabin wall as he rises to close it. Sono and I hold onto the table mounted to the floor and before long, my mentor manages to pull the brace on the window hatch until fastening its cord onto two wooden hooks on its frame. He slides down to the floor off of the wall and crawls to the hatch at the stern which is secured to the rear frame in the same manner.

The cabin door suddenly flings open. Skip and the captain make their way in and manage to secure the door behind them. Skip somehow manages to get one of the lanterns lit. Afterwards, it is realized that Oxer is not with us. Captain Cantik shouts out loud, "Oxer! Where ya be?"

A banging is heard on the cabin door, which skip makes his way to and opens. Oxer stumbles his way in and knocks skip over while Cantik closes and re-secures the door.

Skip becomes annoyed and shouts, "Watch it ya big lummox!"

Oxer holds out his hand and helps Skip to his feet and says, "I'm glad you're alive, mate!" They hug each other while laughing and crying at the same time as the Monsignor manages to secure the third hatch.

The Captain next strips down to his skivvies, throwing his wet cloths over one of many rails which are mounted to the wall. Sitting on his bunk, he says to the Monsignor, "Ha, ha! I see you're getting your sea legs." He looks at us and says, "I'll make sea dogs out of you landlubbers yet!" He covers himself with a blanket and beds down.

We watch the two mates follow suit as Sono asks, "What's next?"

Captain Cantik says while dozing off to sleep, "Shiver me timbers, we ride out the storm of course."

The three of us look at the final bunk and to each other. "I say the monsignor gets it." Sono nods in agreement as the Monsignor says, "Thank you for being kind to an old man."

"Where?" asks Sono.

"I would have to agree with Sono. The way you moved around the cabin to get the hatches shut was no easy task."

Skip says in an impatient tone of voice, "Would you landlubbers settle down? I am trying to get some sleep!

Upon opening my eyes while resting against my pack under a blanket on the table, I realize something is different. The waters are calm. I shout out, "The storm is over!"

"Why are you shouting?" asks Captain Cantik.

Looking down from the sealing, I notice the cabin door to be open before turning my head to see the captain sitting by my side.

The Monsignor looks over from his bunk, sits up, and speaks to us, "Having co-mingled with the seed of the bridegroom as His bride, we are now in agreement with Him under His husbandly authority over us, His spouse. We must always remember standing before Him as He is High Priest and King.

Now, knowing His first love with Him as bridegroom, we can trust Him as King and serve Him out of Love by being His obedient bride. Cantik, I know that you are captain over this vessel, but Christ our Great One as King is Captain over all our vessels. Some vessels are called and some are chosen and He assigns each one of us different positions within His household called the church.

As the Monsignor, I have answered The Bridegroom's call to be chosen and established to have authority over many vessels, not by my own choosing but by The Great One who is King Himself. So, listen very carefully to what I am going to tell you being under His authority from my position.

The attitudes behind our actions spring forth from roots that are grounded in connection with our thoughts, which are either connected to a Spirit that is Holy and full of light or unholy and full of darkness. We have to be very careful to speak from a position of peace in the deciding of what words we shall release from our mouths. For we have a sword on our tongue that speaks darkness or light into existence by what manner of words we choose to allow out of the gate of our mouths to press upon the air. The issues of life or death sprouts as a stem in growth as a key to unlock one of these doors. From now on, we are to examine all of our thoughts and take them captive until we have the focus of a singlemind on The Great One. For when more than one thing captures our vision at a time, there is an open door of opportunity to bring in a confusion which can divide a mind. When there is a darkness that dims vision, mark my words, an enemy from the light of love is there.

Now before there is even the slightest bit of a possibility of looking away from the light of love, I suggest you keep your eyes on The Great One who has just delivered you by understanding His first love towards you. I remind you of the joy that comes from doing the right thing. For afterward, there is the laughter of angels rejoicing through you from the kingdom of heaven."

"I do not always do the right thing, though," says Captain Cantik.

I tell him, "Faint not! For what is impossible with man is possible with God."

"I see now. Although I am helpless, I am not hopeless!"

"Well put," says the Monsignor.

Captain Cantik arrives on the deck smiling as he steps out from the cabin. He calls to his mates, "Oxer, hoist the anchor. Skip, raise the mainsail. The captain takes the wheel as the wind catches the sail and we are soon underway. Stepping out of the cabin to stretch our legs while growing accustomed to the balance of the craft, I next hear Cantik call to us from where he steers, "Ha, ha! I see you three have finally found your sea legs on the *Hope it Floats*."

We wave in response and splitting up, I start to take in the view of the coastal lands while trying to figure out how far we have to go as Sono looks over the bow to observe the nose of the ship cutting through the water.

"Clang! Clang!" The bell chimes and the captain shouts out confirming what I am looking at, "What you are seeing is the desert just beyond the great plains towards the west."

The Monsignor calls to the captain, "That would be the port side."

Captain Cantik calls back, "Argh! You're turning out to be a fine old seadog!"

I then ask, "How much longer do ya figure it will take?"

"We should come upon the Great Forest by noon and pass it before eve. Perhaps we will arrive at our destination by nightfall."

Upon hearing word of the Great Forest, Sono hangs his head. Skip is quick to observe his countenance and shares, "Homesick for the homeland I see."

"I have no desire to return home at this time at all."

"Then why are you so down as we pass the forest if it is of no concern to you?"

"It is more of a concern than you understand, but as the winds can carry our voices…"

"…Perhaps you can fill me in on the details back at the cabin when you care to share more of your story?"

"Let's just say what you learned last night from what was said by the Monsignor is safest for now to know."

"Just remember that as your brother, I am here to share in your burden if you ever have a need for the love of light to push out this darkness as well."

Sono looks over and smiles, "I thank you. From what you have shared, I actually feel a little bit better already."

# The Funeral?

Thomas is preparing himself in preparation of burying the body of Olie when all at once a brilliant little dot of light enters the room from out of nowhere. Suddenly, the light opens up forming an angel, shining with a light with a glow that takes the form of a man and lights up the room. He drops his prayer book to the floor as his mouth opens wide.

The procession stands waiting at the gravesite for Thomas to arrive and begins to wonder why he is taking so long. Ceasil, Olies father, says to Suma while standing before the body wrapped in a burial shroud in the heat of the day, "Some priest they have chosen for us. Such disrespect as to show up late for our funeral." Suma begins to weep. Bowing her head, she holds up her hands and covers her face.

"We shall not have a burial today," says Thomas, who arrives carrying a scroll he has just penned out.

Ceasil says angrily, "First, you disrespect us by arriving late and now you jest us!"

"I meant no disrespect. Ceasil, you are to take this scroll to Bartholomew at the Monastery that your son may live."

"You further insult us after apologizing! We have no further use for your services, priest."

Suma falls to her husband's feet and looks up at him through her tear-filled eyes and says, "Please do as he says!"

Ceasil turns to their leader and asks, "What saith you, Trevor?"

"You are letting your anger get in the way of The Great One's mercy by your judgment."

Looking over to the priest, Ceasil takes the scroll and waterskin which Thomas offers and starts for the monastery.

Trevor asks, "What would you have us do, Thomas?"

"I was instructed to preserve the body in salt water. There is a feeding trough in the store house where I am staying. Place the body there and we shall fill it with water and add salt.

Trevor further inquires, "Who instructed you?"

Thomas responds with a smile, "An angel, of course."

A five o'clock sun rests on the horizon at eve as the inlet to a river appears.

Ding! Ding! "There she be, the mouth of the Dailey River. The next stop for *Hope it Floats* is the mountains of Dagog," says Captain Cantik.

Steering hard to port, he calls out to his second mate, "Oxer, take the sounding pole and see how deep the waters be. Skip, give him a hand as you know how troubled these waters can be. Just as Skip grabs the pole, the boat begins to rock in the tide. We hear the captain's voice in the background, "Monsignor, Marcus, Sono! It'd be best if you three went inside the cabin. As Sono makes his way from the bow towards the stern, the pole swoops over his head. When I enter the cabin, the Monsignor is already sitting at the table. The boat suddenly bounces on the current and I lose my footing. If not for the bar on the wall to grab onto, I would have fallen to the floor. Sono comes bouncing in through the door and slides across the room before grabbing a hold of a bench which is bolted to the floor. Our craft suddenly escapes the pull from the tide and heads straight for rocks that jut out of the water at a point just inside the inlet.

Some divine timing allows the sounding pole to be in position for Oxer to extend the pole into a rock and cast us off the shore line as we sail past the jetty and into the river. There is no time to take a sounding, so Cantik steers the *Hope it Floats* towards the center of the river and hopes for the best.

Ceasil stands and takes a last drink of water before approaching the door to the monastery. He starts using the polished brass knocker and awaits a response.

The door keeper's voice is heard, "On what business do you come to the monastery?"

"Thomas sent me to deliver a scroll."

After a brief wait, the door opens and he is bid to come in. "I have come to see Bartholomew."

Following the guide past the floral garden and through the open courtyard, they enter a large building complex. Sitting at a visitors station is brother Jerome. He further guides as Ceasil follows right beside him with opened eyes. He takes in the sight of paintings which hang on the walls along with some quaint reading areas that contain a wealth of books 'til finally arriving before two oak doors where Jerome comes to a stop.

With the thought of books still on the mind of Ceasil, he ponders out loud, "I do not know how to read. Do you know if the note I bear can be read to me?"

Jerome looks over with a friendly smile and says, "Have faith," then knocks on the door to the study.

"You may enter."

Upon entry, Ceasil rushes forward with his note in hand and holds it before Bartholomew who sits at the cherrywood desk in Monsignor's seat and asks, "Can you read it to me?"

Bartholomew opens the scroll and begins to read it to himself then says out loud, "Oh my!"

"Can you please read it to me?"

"You would be Ceasil?"

"That I would."

"Let faith in The Great One be the greater desire for you at this time." Turning to Jerome, he asks him to go into his quarters, the Monsignor's room, and to bring out their messenger. "I must prepare this note for travel." After folding it over into quarters, he places it into a little red box with a band around it while Jerome returns with a rather large golden eagle, which is perched upon a leather armband he has fastened to his forearm.

After fastening the small red box to the eagle's leg, they walk to the back of the room to a window with closed shutters.

Ceasil realizes, "You're not going to tell me what's in the note, are you?"

Jerome responds while Bartholomew opens the shutters, "All things are possible for those who believe."

The two say at the same time while the eagle is released into the night sky, "Have faith!"

The three watch from the window as the eagle ascends into the darkness until it disappears from sight. Bartholomew closes the shutters and as he turns, he sees Ceasil looking up and then beyond. "My faith flies to the kingdom of heaven, just as your eagle flies into the night sky. This is where my trust lies."

The sun glares off the water of the Dailey River. Cracks of light seep through the cabin of the *Hope it Floats*. Captain Cantik gets up from his bunk and walks to the cabin door. After unlatching it, he pushes it open with a creak to a flood of light which comes pouring in upon us and disrupts our rest. "Time to rise and shine, mates. Skip, breakout the fishing gear. For the sooner ya do, the sooner we breakfast.

Now, if you three landlubbers want to officially become seadogs, you are gonna have to learn to fish. Oxer here is the best there is when it comes to teaching how to fish. He even taught me and Skip a few things. So if ya listen up, you'll catch on quick."

I sit up on the table while saying, "Did you not learn the other day that man doth not live by bread alone but by every word which proceeds out of the mouth of God, which is living food as well?"

"Everyone knows that fish always bite best in the morning."

"This is the day that the Lord has made, let us rejoice and be glad. If The Great One made the fish, is it not possible that if we honor Him, He can make anything possible, including a catch of fish?"

Sono comments, "Why can't we honor God when we fish? I for one want to learn what Oxer has to teach."

I turn to my mentor and ask, "Monsignor, what do you have to say about all this?"

Sitting up in his bunk, he responds by nodding his head and saying, "I see that I am inquired of first thing this morn… It is a good thing this is an easy answer."

"What do you mean?" asks Captain Cantik.

"It all depends on who has the highest authority as the true captain who keeps this ship afloat. Yet, I will still leave the decision up to you."

# Arrival of the Golden Eagle

The eagle comes out of the sun while in flight with splashes of gold upon its feathers. It glides down to an open castle window and walks on its ledge before it is discovered by a voice which speaks softly to it, "Well, what brings you here?"

A youthful looking gray haired old gentleman holds out a leather armband on his forearm to which the bird responds with a flutter and a perch. As he rests upon his arm, a knock is heard at the door to his chambers.

"Most noble healer, may I come in?"

"You most certainly may, Prince Liam."

As the door opens, the healer responds, "I see the arrival of our friend has not gone unnoticed."

"What news doth he bring?"

"I was just about to find out." Taking a piece of seeded bread from his pocket, he sets the eagle upon a wooden perch and proceeds to feed it. He continues to speak in a soothing tone of voice, "Well, my friend, what do you have for me?"

He unties the little red box from its leg and removes the note before opening it.

Another knock is heard at the open doorway, "Come in Edward," says Prince Liam.

The healer hands the note over, "It's for you, Liam."

Knock, knock! "I heard word…"

"…Well, Ashley. How nice to see you. This is becoming a popular spot. Majesty, I suggest you take your note to court before it gets too crowded in here."

Prince Liam looks to the eagle with a nod, "Thank you, my fine feathered friend." The three then exit the room and leave the healer to himself.

Bartholomew is sitting in the Monsignor's seat before the desk back at the monastery. Ceasil sits opposite him with open ears that are attentive to listen. "How would you like to learn to read, Ceasil?"

"You have my interest."

"I withheld the information in the note to give this interest along with your faith. For I want you to know from this time forth that faith and reason must come together in order to see the light of truth in its full brilliance. This must be known ahead of time, for not everything which is read will add to the brilliance of The Great One. This is why we are going to teach you to read from a book called the *Book of Life*. For once you know the truth of light, you will be able to tell when something you read is not of it. This is called discernment. Once learning to rightly divide the word of truth, you will also be able to tell when something is off in the word of truth from The Great One's meaning, which will enhance your life as well.

If you are willing, Ceasil, because of the humble and uncorrupted position you now have, a choice to become chosen has been granted to you."

"I am willing to do whatever it takes to walk through the door of light and become the Great One's child."

"Good, for now I can tell you more."

"What more is there to know than becoming a child of light?"

"Two can set ten thousand to flight. For mankind is not alone here on earth. There are fallen angels that hide in darkness and like to take advantage of those who remain in the dimness of the breadth, which passes through the heights and depths of time."

"This is more than I know."

"Hereafter, you shall become more familiar with glory light. For when man is by himself, he is more vulnerable to attack from what is dark within his soul. Beware, for inside the length of time, they rise out from the abyss to blind us from our thoughts, which guards evil's destruction from our souls. They are there in the depths that remain unseen as they interfere by rising up in our emotions to overwhelm us as well."

"What is it you are speaking of?"

"By not knowing how to sense these dragon angels that feast upon our souls, we're manipulated into anxiety without the gift of God's control. For we get stung with death in each choice of reach in place of the life of serving Him. Every grasp from a lack of calling out to the One who can deliver invites an inward shout and sinks us deeper in the trap of not getting out. Yes, blinded by them - these fallen spirits that seduce our flesh with all their charm when not aware that they are there. For neither do we see them in our thoughts when dimness keeps us prisoners to the breadth 'til finally stilled. Yes, they prevent any emotions or thoughts from coming into balance between our hearts and minds. Then keeping us irritable in souls, we just survive while remaining blind. Though once faith lights with reason, we can remember to call and keep our hands from reaching into the belly of the abyss instead of God's love, which from birth we were trained to miss as we continually got bit. Not by loving parents you may say, but in their youths, they've been seduced into being trained in the very same way."

"You just saved me from turning to wine to ease the pain of the loss of my son. For I see that there is a new hope by those who trust in a God who is greater, even than death."

"No, one man can become aware of this alone. For as iron sharpens iron, so doth the countenance of a good friend when seeing with reason in a faith that brings to light all that's dark. For this reason, I want to train you to be a friend and right hand to the priest that neither of you shall have to stand alone. Eternal life must take root in you and become your home or salvation's purpose will not take place as all of creation is interconnected."

"I have a wife."

"Splendid! I will send for her, too. You will be pillars of the community and strengthen the priest by bearing much more of a reflection to Christ in all. There will be a safe haven for everyone."

"You are very wise."

"Then you agree. It is settled. The two of you will call upon the hand of God together. Sparks of light will fly from heat of sword. Where two or more are gathered in His name there The Great One will be in your midst to put out darkness by His light. Remember, though. He can only deliver when you remain in His light that doth not fade. Stay in this moment when you see to call upon Him and you will not sink in waves that slowly drown you. For He will bear you up above the spirit beast and keep you out of the heat of its reach."

"What will my training entail?"

"A full understanding of the New Covenant, how to rightly divide the word of truth so you can report back to me or the Monsignor if anything seems off in the church, and administrative duties. For as The Great One blesses your community, you will want to help out the less fortunate from your abundance in the storehouse, too."

"I see that I still have much to learn after all."

A gentle knocking is heard at the door. "Are there any further questions?"

"How is all this going to be paid for?"

"It is more blessed to be able to give than receive. For those who understand not to give begrudgingly, great becomes their reward."

There is another knock, "One moment please!"

"Ceasil, I want you to report to Jerome who first brought you here, he will get you set up."

"Thank you, Bartholomew."

"Just remember to always keep your thanksgiving in your heart towards The Great One, for a grateful heart will keep you lit and what lurks in darkness out."

Ceasil nods while getting up from his chair as he receives final instruction from Bartholomew, "Please show my guests in on your way out."

The gentle knock is heard again as he gets up, but when he goes to the door, no one is there. "Do you have any invisible friends?"

We hear the knocking again. Bartholomew says, "The window!"

"The Window?"

"It seems we have a reply from the castle."

"Castle?"

"Have you not heard of Calington Castle?"

Ceasil shakes his head *no*.

"I will show you the map of our region, but first, would you open the shutters while I put on my armband?"

Ceasil goes to the shutters while Bartholomew lifts the leather band from his desk and follows behind as he puts it on. The shutters are opened and the eagle hops in from the ledge and onto the band. Holding it up on his arm, he turns to Ceasil and says while walking to his desk, "Our eagle has arrived."

# Dagog

Dropping the longboat in the water with a splash, it is drawn back alongside the *Hope it Floats* by two ropes tied from its bow and stern. Oxer climbs down into the longboat and braces himself in the center. Extending his arms, he steadies a wagon with a pull handle containing two large empty water barrels that are lowered on a small hoist which is mounted on the deck of the ship. Steading the rig with his hand, he lowers it into the boat on a platform at its center before tying it down.

Once the wagon and barrels are firmly secured, Oxer calls out, "Ready for passengers!"

Captain Cantik gives instruction, "Skip, stay on the ship and let nothing on it. Man, bird, or beast."

"Aye-aye, captain."

"In fact, make do with the supplies you have in the galley and do not fish, for that Chaffie fella is pretty crafty with his sorcery. Fetch me bow and a quiver full of arrows and be on the ready with yours. Oxer and I should be back by nightfall. There should be some game and freshwater on our return."

Skip goes to the cabin and unhooks a bow and a quiver full of arrows before placing them on the table and returns for more. Captain Cantik helps us board by using an oar. Once we are secure, he joins us after passing down the other. While returning, Skip tosses him the bow first and then the quiver as Oxer places the oars in their locks while taking position.

Cantik instructs Sono, "Untie the skiff from the stern while I undo the bow."

Sono replies, "Aye, captain!"

Now free of the ship, Oxer casts off from the side with an oar. As we glide, he begins to row for the shore of Dagog.


Morris, Manfried, and Gyus are sitting on board the wagon that originally brought the dwarfs, Bartholomew, and I. Ceasil sits on the front alongside Nettle who is holding the reins as Manfried speaks out to all in the wagon, "We must prepare our hearts for what we are going to see this day. For the Creator is going to visit us today. Prince Liam's hands will be used to breathe the breath of life into the dark recesses of death by The Great One's heart of light that shall feel and grieve through love.

Ceasil shares what is on his heart, "I do not know of such things. I can only hope and trust according to all your stories that the God I long to experience for myself will move and bring healing to my heart. Just from what I understand, He has pricked my love with His affections that comfort me." Tears meet with the father's eyes as he begins to weep 'til he is like a river run dry. They are now parted as The Great One's Spirit is on him as a wind upon water, which refashions him into a smile at the acknowledgement of His presence.

Nettle looks over and notices and says, "He is smiling!"

"I could not believe that my teeth would ever show again and yet they are as my tears have dried. No matter what happens now, I can praise God for His goodness in any situation.

On the fields before the Dailey River with Dagog off in the distance, a dwarf ducks his head in the trench. Chaffie remains hidden from sight as he passes by the church town which was established from the time when the truth was being tested.

The sun shifts in the sky. After his journey, he steps off the fields before the Dailey River when he notices the *Hope it Floats* in the midst of its waters and becomes curious. Looking to the skies, he observes some seagulls. They squawk at the water before swooping down to snatch up a fish. He tarries for a time and continues to watch the sky. Chaffie next sees what he has been waiting for. A mature bald eagle swoops down and snatches a gull in its claws with fish in tow. He sings out to the large winged creature, "Bird of feather, be friend to this dwarf. Come down upon me now and carry me across."

The eagle ascends from the sky and hovers over Chaffie and drops its prey, which falls on his head. He rolls his eyes and braces himself as the great bird comes down on his shoulders and lifts him, taking him up in the air as he begins to be carried over the river.

Onboard the *Hope it Floats,* Skip is on the watch. At first he's taken aback, but then realizes what is happening. With bow in hand after removing an arrow from his quiver, he takes aim, draws back his bow, and fires on Chaffie. Missing him, he hits the eagle which drops the dwarf into the water.

Chaffie cries out in the water from the shock of the cold and realizes he is drowning. While barely staying afloat, he chants at the wind, "Friend to fish, I will always be. Come fin, meet my hand and snatch me up from under my knees." A large dorsal fin appears in the water. Then the fish swims underneath his knees, lifting him from out of his predicament as he grabs its fin which meets with his hand.

Skip's jaw drops open at the sight. He quickly reloads his bow and anticipates where he is going to appear on shore and steadies himself on the boat which bobs in the river.

He's out in the shallows, a clean shot. The bow is released, but as the arrow sings through the air, Chaffie trips on the last wave landing on the beach as the arrow passes over him. The dwarf quickly makes a fist and blows on it 'til opening his hand, which he suddenly thrusts towards the ship. As Skip goes to reload, he is caught by a violent wind which rocks the boat. He manages to get off a shot, but it falls shy and sticks out from the sand as Chaffie disappears into the brush and takes cover in the tall grass just off the beach.

Captain Cantik and Oxer appear on the trail, returning with supply for the ship. The first mate pulls the wagon while the captain pushes from behind. A deer lays atop of the now filled water barrels, but they manage to keep it moving along.

Then he sees it, an arrow sticking out from the beach halfway in the sand with fresh little footprints leading into the brush. This causes Cantik to stop and look towards the *Hope it Floats* where he sees Skip gesturing at something in the brush next to him. Oxer continues to move the wagon onto the beach on his own and doth not realize that the captain has drawn an arrow to scan the brush. The wagon rolls easier on the beach as the sand has turned firm and with the longboat dead ahead, he turns to trade places with his captain and notices he is not there. The captain shouts to Oxer, "Get the longboat loaded, I have some hunting to tend to!"

Chaffie sees Cantik from the middle of the field within the brush. Tossing a little pebble which makes a noise causes the captain to release his arrow at a bush that moves.

"I know you're out there, Chaffie!" shouts the captain.

Chaffie throws his voice to the other side of the field, "I don't even know you. Why come after me?" His voice is heard near the woods and away from his present location, which causes a rapid fire of a succession of arrows to try and stop him. "So, it's cat and mouse is it?" Throwing his voice again further back in the field causes a release of two more arrows.

"The question is who is the cat and who is the mouse?" He throws his voice again, only this time rather than shoot his arrow, Cantik advances into the field to flush out the dwarf. Rather than wait for him to approach for a better shot, Chaffie suddenly darts towards the forest with his right foot and zig-zags back on his left which causes an arrow to spin off his side and graze him when released. With his last arrow run out, he dashes in the opposite direction towards the beach as Chaffie continues to head towards the forest. Seeing the arrow sticking out of the sand on the beach, Captain Cantik grabs it in hand, but when he goes to take aim, the dwarf disappears into the woods.

A wounded Chaffie looks out through the foliage while undercover and watches as the captain returns to help finish loading the longboat before getting back to the ship. Checking the seriousness of his stinging wound, he realizes that he has only been nicked, but searches around for some plantain weed to cover his wound all the same. He finally finds some in a patch of sun showing through the forest about ten yards away. After tearing a leaf, he quickly chews some into a sauve and places it on another, which he places over his open wound before covering it with what is left of his sash. The thought enters his mind, *"After getting back to the ship, will they get more arrows and come track me?"* He goes back to the ship to investigate and discovers that the longboat has been raised from the water.

Feeling more relaxed, he sits back beneath a tree and reclines to rest himself.

# Resurrection

The Sun hangs four o'clock over the village of Ostrog as the wagon carrying Ceasil, Olie's father, and the others approaches.

Prince Liam, along with his wife Ashley, and his brother Prince Edward, ride their horses with hearts full of life.

From reading the note attached to the golden eagle, Prince Liam looks up from a small map he has penned while coming out of the mountains of Zantee, "See there on the horizon? According to my calculations, that should be the village of Ostrog."

"Then let us go there, my brother."

Ashley follows prayerfully along as know-ing what is to come from being prepared by deep meditation concerning all. She humbles herself in

the reflection of a song that they may abound in the
Spirit while they ride:

> Come let us sing,
>
> come let us dance and sing,
>
> unto the Lord who is our Christ, and only King.

> Come let us sing,
>
> come let us dance and sing,
>
> Christ… is… Lord.

> He is our light,
>
> which pierced our minds of dark,
>
> with warmth of love,
>
> when we were falling apart.

> He brought us life,
>
> while death was at our door.
>
> For as we searched,
>
> His taste was not ignored.

It was our quest
to find a way to live
that we could breathe,
the breath of all, e-ter-nity.

Now we are one,
as we have seen the king.
He is the door
which causes us to sing.

We are alive,
when time is spent with Him.
Eternal babes, because of what He did.

Now we have grown,
to know the way to go.
A brilliant glory,
You shine within our eyes.

Exalted King, who paved the way for us.
You alone, have paid the pre-cious cost.
Remaining free,
when bowed upon our knees

Our actions tell,
of all the good You bring,
with words so sweet,
just like a gentle dove.


Come let us sing,
come let us dance and sing,
unto the Lord who is our Christ, and only King.


Come let us sing,
come let us dance and sing,
Christ… is… Lord!


After she finishes singing, a wagon is seen approaching in a diverging direction. We can tell that our destinations are going to meet outside the village.

"Liam, do you see…"

"…Yeah, I see them."


Not far from the wagon, Nettle notices three horses with riders drawing near and calls out to his passengers in the back, "Manfried, I see some riders with emblems on their horse blankets on the approach to the village. Two of them are men bearing swords and the third one be a lady."

"Would one of the emblems be a lion on a shield?"

"Why, yes."

"Ride over towards them, nice and slow."

"But what about my son in the village?" says Ceasil.

"You might as well get acquainted with the one who is going to raise your son because one of the two men is probably Prince Liam."

"Hey, I've heard that name before from Bartholomew when he was showing me the map of the province in the Monsignor's office." Turning his head, he looks back at the priest, "He's come a long way to meet me. I for one would like to ride in with him. Thank you for telling me, Manfried."

Very well then," says Nettle as he slows the wagon.


Prince Edward says to his two riding companions, "It looks like we are in for some company."

"Prince Liam nods and responds, "If I know the timing of The Great One, the boy's father is probably the passenger up in the front who is smiling at us."

The riders and the traveling wagon meet and start to head towards the village together. Manfried calls out, "Prince Liam, it has been a long while. Why not tie your horse and ride with us so that you might get better acquainted with the father of the boy you are going to raise up as he yet rides with us?"

"It sounds like a plan."

Onboard the *Hope it Floats* in the waters before Dagog, Captain Cantik and his crew are having a discussion about Chaffie being a possible threat to Sono, the Monsignor, and I.

Skip advises, "After seeing what I saw of Chaffie's powers, I say to let the priests handle them."

The captain responds by saying, "Now, you must not be intimidated by any who has use of earthly powers. Remember what the Monsignor had said, 'Greater is He that is in us than he that is in the world.' Besides, the priests may not have to handle him either as pinning him down and wounding him earlier has slowed this dwarf down quite a bit, allowing our passengers a good head start. Caffie might not even catch up with them now. With eve almost upon us, I am sure he is resting his wounds."

All arrive at the well from their travels. While getting water, they are noticed by a villager who informs, Trevor.  He in turn sends him to Thomas before going out to meet those at the well.

Prince Liam looks up from taking a drink of water out of a bucket with a ladle and sees the town elder who introduces himself, "To whom do I have the pleasure of meeting this eve?"

"My name is Liam, this is Ashley, my wife, and brother Edward. Now, to whom do I have the pleasure of meeting?"

"I would be…"

"…Trevor, these good people are here to help Olie!" says Ceasil excitedly.

"Prince Liam!" shouts Thomas. "Glory be to God for getting you here so quickly."

"My son is not far from here," Ceasil volunteers.

"Come, Prince Liam, the boy awaits your touch," says Thomas.

Prince Liam follows after Thomas, followed by an entourage of Ceasil and everyone else. News spreads like wildfire throughout the village and soon everyone is standing outside or inside the storehouse.

After praying, Prince Liam looks to the crowd, "Why have you come? What has caused your hearts to bring you here?"

The crowd remains silent as Olie's father, Prince Edward, and Ashley look on. He continues, "Well, what if I were to tell you that you are here because you search for something which is real? Know it now. The Great One is more than real. For He had said, 'I am the resurrection and I have come to give you a life of abundance that will last for an eternity as I am eternal life.'"

Looking to the boy's father, Prince Liam says, "Now, so you may know that The Great One keeps his promises and is more than real as He is life, watch with me!" He looks down at Olie's wrapped body in the feeding trough under water and says, "In the name of Jesus Christ of Nazareth, be raised up."

Olie sits up out of the water while in the shroud as Liam continues, "Be not troubled or afraid, for the mind is kept at perfect peace when stayed on

Thee. Now, would someone unwrap him so he can get out of this water?"

The father rushes over and lifts his son out of the water while his mother starts unwrapping him.

The crowd looks on full of smiles and has expressions of wonderment.

Liam bows his head and raises his arms and says, "I love You, Great One. You are my God and I worship You alone!"

Ashley continues to pray while Prince Edward says to the crowd, "Let our hearts always be true."

There are a lot of solemn amens.

Prince Liam brings down his arms as Olie, now fully clothed and standing before the crowd, addresses them, "I was in a wonderful place, one where I met with The Great One's love. Yet I found it more important to return to you, my people, and encourage your faith."

Trevor announces, "I for one am encouraged." After a moment of silence, he begins to clap his hands. The crowd gradually joins in 'til it thunders up to heaven.

Shouts of praise are next heard as their voices are captured by the wind in a chorus of, "Praise be to The Great One!"

Olie looks over at the crowd and smiles.

# Family Reunion

It is just getting dark when the Monsignor and the others see a light coming from the house adjoined to the cave of his prior visit. As not to take his sisters by surprise, the Monsignor calls out, "Hello!"

A figure appears in the window, "Doth that be you, brother?"

"Yes, Claire. It be me."

Some other shadowy figures pass by the window. Afterwards, the door opens as we approach. The Monsignor bids for us to wait by the steps at the foot of the porch. He then goes and warmly greets his sisters one by one with hugs of affection. They respond by kissing his cheeks and with words of how they've missed him. "Is it really you?" is heard from where Sono and I stand. It brings me joy to watch their warm and loving greeting. It is hard to believe that they practiced the craft of evil so ruth-lessly without mercy, even to the point of wanting to take each other's life. I tell Sono of some of the stories I have heard 'til finally we are introduced.

"This be Marcus, my very knowledgeable apprentice. With him is our traveling companion, Sono. It seems the Great One has him along to learn a few things that might end up being invaluable to his people, speaking of which, are under the spell of the charm stone by Katrina's old apprentice, Chaffie, who is now a full warlock dwarf.

Claire speaks for herself and all of her sisters, "This sounds very serious. You all better come in and pray with us right away."

Stepping into their charmingly quaint cottage entrance, we see chairs, which we place our packs, a table for eating, and preparation area. After being made to feel at home, we find ourselves in a prayer circle on a large round rug upon the floor.

Joining hands, Claire leads us, "Great One, I ask for your protection over our home. Put up a wall of defense of fifty yards around this house so evil cannot get through and secure us now in your firm position."

Sister Ezmarelda is next to pray, "Lord, soften Chaffie's heart so he may come out from darkness and embrace the warmth of Your love as You've done for me within You as light."

Nilda, another sister, prays, "Let this dwarf not be able to disguise himself in a lie as to the truth of His character. Keep him honest with us that we might address any dark areas within his life."

Zena, the last and final sister prays, "Allow him to discover us so we may implement my sister's prayers to You in Your timing. For I acknowledge that You must build Your house or everything will be in vain."

The Monsignor prays next, "I acknowledge my sister's wisdom and agree with them in prayer…"

"…as do I," says Sono and I at the same time. All of us then join in with a hearty, "Amen!"

The Monsignor says to Nilda who is sitting next to him, "Phew! What did you eat?"

"Ha! Brother, do you not remember when our inner self expresses itself outwardly? It is as a door to another world."

"Unfortunately, I do."

Sono excuses himself, "I need some fresh air." As he gets up to leave, I follow him out.

"Some family, huh?" says Sono.

"What do you mean?"

"All that prayer wisdom and still their flesh doth not die. Seeing how God's mercy endures forever gives me great hope. With the vision they just gave me of how God is faithful to bring to completion that good work in which he has started in us is a real encouragement to me and a testimony of His perfection."

"I am glad that you see it this way as mercy always triumphs over judgment and brings the light of life in place of death and its darkness."

"Marcus!"

"What happened to your voice, Sono?"

He responds, "I didn't say anything."

"Marcus, it is you! Thank the heavens and of course, The Great One."

"Bolo? Is that you?"

"You've remembered!"

"What brings you all the way out here?"

"I had nowhere else to go. For in knowing that the sisters are powerful children of the light as we now call them, I was coming to them for help, but now you're here from out of nowhere. It must be The Great One's timing, it has to be."

"Help from what? And why are you away from your people as their leader?"

"I have the gift of the loudest voice, which allows others to hear me. As for my leadership, a council has been left in charge while I am away, which is a part of our protocol as a people..

Next is my order of business at hand that will explain why I'm here. Puppco, whom you brought into the caverns with you, has become overpowered by spirits of fallen angels…"

"We'd better go inside as we have problems of our own and it might not be safe to talk outside."

I know of the spirits of the wind, which carry voices to the evil one and those who do its bidding, too. If you do not mind helping me up these stairs, I would like to go in with you."

Marcus walks down the steps from the porch and lowers his hand to the ground, which Bolo who is two inches tall climbs into.

Sono asks, "What kind of being are you?"

"I am a gnome."

"I didn't know that there were people shorter than us dwarfs."

"Well, did you know fairies are even shorter than us?"

"Oh, yeah! I bet you never saw an elf."

"Would you two stop it?" I open the door and we enter back in.

Upon entering, the Monsignor is instructing his sisters, "We can partake of all things, but not all things are profitable in our relationship with The Great One. For certain things from our past can get in the way of knowing Him better. I am glad that we had the chance to do some reminiscing to see this more clearly. Ah, I see that Marcus has returned with our traveling companion."

I say while raising my hand, "Make that two companions now."

"My name is Bolo. As the leader of the gnomes, I am at your service. Only I need your help now."

"What would you like us to do for you, Bolo?" asks the Monsignor.

"I have started to tell Marcus outside already that on his previous adventure he had with Puppco, who is a member from my tribe. Well, he is under some demonic activity and all is not well. For that deep sleep which had fallen on him before you left turned out to be an invasion of dark angel offspring entering into his mind. It must have happened before you returned from the caves when getting the serum of the righteous root."

"Which I can confirm, Monsignor, as I was with him."

"Well after you had gone, he awoke along with many of these demons, which function through him. They thrash him and others about who have tried to approach him to help. Becoming fearful, I have seen my people add strength to the spirits possessing him as they get even stronger by the energy of their fears while we yet speak.

I came here to see if they can be cast out and have Puppco restored."

"Yes, it can be done," says the Monsignor.

"Afterwards, I will reward you with some information about the elf witch that is among Sono's people. Please, this is an urgent matter!"

The Monsignor becomes angry, "I do not make deals!"

I become involved, "But I know this gnome personally and feel an obligation for us to take action."

"No deal. For we are already on a mission to close the door on evil when we discover just how to do it. You know as well as I that we are working against a spell which needs to be broken for the dwarf people already."

Feeling empowered, I make a stand, "Then I will go on with Bolo along with anyone else who would come with me without you."

Sono says, "Could we not do this along the way?"

The Monsignor continues to stand his ground as well, "We will be heading in the opposite direction. For if I remember my geography, they are down near the valley of the land of the giant insects and we are headed towards the mountains. A trap of some sort must be set by the lower realm before Chaffie arrives to stop him from getting there at least. We must try to close this door on evil. Time is an urgent matter as there is no telling how near he might be already."

Claire offers some advice, "No worry there, brother, as Chaffie, being an old and dear acquaintance to us, would stop here first for at least a meal."

Her family agrees, "You are right."

Sono says, "I do not want to go anywhere near a land of giant insects. Count me out!"

There is now a further dispute between the Monsignor and I as my mentor suggests, "Exorcism is a two-man operation so that the spirits do not jump on the man who is performing it as there is the danger of a strong spiritual pride that can enter in."

"I do not care what you know or for how long you've known it. When you do not take the time to even look at me when you talk, you treat me as a stranger. For when I was at the monastery, you barely looked at me and now you want me to respect that your words are in line with your actions. I have seen how you treat your sisters in comparison to me. Without even knowing it, you try to put things on me like I was that table over there. Please try to talk to me and not at me so there might be a true rational protocol of a love which will bond our relationship from now on. For we need to have the respect of a full measure of joy in each other's company in place of what we now have."

"No point to prove on my part as God meets everyone at their own pace within a timing He sees fit for each of us. What you said was well spoken, but dealing with Chaffie is the greater threat of evil right now."

Claire makes a suggestion, "Why not take care of Chaffie first and then cast the fallen angels out of the gnome?"

The Monsignor answers his sister, "You are filled with excellent ideas this night, sis. I can even set a trap for Chaffie, which would take away his powers in a prayer zone that we could grab and restrain him. Afterwards, as my sister suggested, we could drive these demons out of the gnome that you know. Well, how doth it sound, Marcus?"

Bolo in his desperation speaks to the sisters, "Maybe you could come and help while they are in the mountains by the lower realm."

Zena speaks up, "We would break faith with The Great One by not honoring Him if we do not wait for an answer to our prayer requests. Wait and see. Everything comes to pass in the Lord's timing for those who are patient."

The gnome fesses up, "Well, if this be the case, I must tell you what I know about the elf witch among your people, Sono."

"What do you know?"

"The elf witch is really Bashna's wife who disappeared during Katrina's reign in the forest. Ella is really Bella and she has a spell on her. She was used as a decoy. So, while people were wondering about her, Chaffie would have free reign behind the scenes. The only way to break the spell is for her to drink the serum from the righteous root."

"How did you know this?" asks Sono.

"You are not the only one with a past. Before I knew the Great One, I was hired by Chaffie to place this spell on her."

The Monsignor speaks with his eyes enlightened, "What if I were to tell everyone that we must keep watch for spirits by keeping our eyes on The Great One at all times and persevere for as long as possible 'til it becomes second nature while here on earth as it is in heaven?"

"I would say you are treating us like a father doth his own family like my old mentor did."

In knowing him, you were able to make a comparison to me. You will learn a lot from doing this with others as well, but most importantly, you must learn of our Great One and Christ who is perfection. We need to compare all others with Him when we are unsure of whether or not we can trust others in any given situation in life. Then should we ourselves fall short, we need to pray for God's wisdom to change us into His likeness that we may go from glory to glory by the craft of His Spirit while in our various stages of communing growth."

My mentor holds a vile of serum before Sono. "This is why you're here with us. Go and free Bella and she in turn will free your people when talking to Bashna. For he will find her love more valuable than the charm he now possesses. It will be the beginning of the breaking of the spell on him and your people.

While we do battle against the evil that is in Chaffie, a sign will be given to you which you'll not be able to deny as everyone in the tribe will do it at the same time. This is when Bashna must make a decree as you will instruct him to have everyone throw their stones into the fire pit at the central clearing in the forest. They must do it right away, for I do not know how long I can wrestle with Chaffie in the prayer zone before he gets out of the trap and have his powers restored. Long after we've left for the mountains, my sisters will delay Chaffie whenever he arrives by offering him a meal to give us extra time. Then through using the light of wisdom, present him with another opportunity to work his seductive magic against The Great One's character. By the time he discovers there be no breaching the Holy Spirit while on the Lord's path, nor desire for earthly pleasures from the gratification of any pride within them, we should be in position.

This will not concern you, though. By this time, Captain Cantik will be taking you across the Dailey River. Make no stops along the way. If all goes well in two days' time, you shall see the sign within your tribe."

"But what if they do not listen to me?"

"Have Bashna throw his stone in fire, which you will build first and the rest of your tribe will follow."

"How will I know the sign again?"

"It will be an action that all your fellow dwarfs will do at the same time, which you shall easily recognize. Now have faith, for the great one will be with you."

You mean I am to leave right now?"

The Monsignor nods his head and with that, Sono takes up his pack and with a few farewells bid, he starts on his way.

I raise my voice from across the room and say, "We'll be praying for you."

# Sono's Encounter

Making his way down the trail that brought him up the mountain seems a lot easier under the cover of night without full light of heat on the pack he bears. He doth not feel alone either, for the thought, *"We'll be praying for you,"* stays with him, making him more aware that the presence of The Great One is there.

Eyes look out at the *Hope it Floats* through the foliage of the woods. It is seen anchored in the river. A light comes from its cabin and by this light, the viewer sees a watch has been posted with bow and arrow overlooking the beach. Then it dawns on Chaffie, *"There must be passengers that are going to return to the ship!"* He checks his wound and realizes the bleeding has stopped by moonlight.

He looks around for a big stick until he finds just the right one he can use for a club. Handling it with swings, he checks its balance before starting off for the main trail.

The Monsignor and I start out as well after packing special rigs in our packs and placing spare boots on our feet for rough hiking. It is a good thing that Nilda's boots fit me and Claire's her brothers. Saying goodbye to his sisters, we close the door behind us and start on our way. Bolo rides in the pocket of my robe while standing on a handkerchief with his head sticking out for air as we walk the night.

Chaffie quickly hikes the trail at a brisk pace while looking for places to set a trap. As it grows cooler before dawn, he becomes more aggressive in his pace. He starts to see shadows from mountain peaks with flashes of glimmering light from a rising sun which flashes through them. All at once, he sees Sono walking towards him in a grassy area of the pass with woods on either side. Raising his club, he charges forward and while yelling, he brings down his weapon towards Sono's head. Dodging the heavy stick, it catches the corner of his brow and he falls down and lands on the pack. When Chaffie raises the club a second time to take advantage of him being on the ground, Sono calls out, "Help me, oh Great One!" A bear suddenly advances towards the aggression of this warlock's dwarf forward-thrusting arm and catches him by surprise. Seeing the bear too late to try and spell him, Chaffie starts to run up the path deeper into the mountains.

Sono staggers to his feet and continues on his way to the river 'til falling down but manages to get up and advance towards the ship.

While we are walking, the terrain starts getting rough which makes me grateful of the Lord's provision of the boots I wear. Our breaths are now that of cool vapors which grow longer after a few hours of travel. We soon reach an area where it becomes difficult to walk without falling back. Seeing many paths to choose from to further advance up the mountains, we determine this is the best place to set the prayer-foot trap.

Looking up towards heaven, the Monsignor calls on the The Great One as I join hands in agreement with Him, "Lord, I ask that wherever my feet shall tread, no evil thing will be able to set foot upon the ground as it will be holy unto thy name."

After breaking from prayer, we slowly start to cover the ground with our tracks one step at a time starting at the entire base of the mountains.

An exhausted Chaffie, finally being able to elude the bear, soon discovers the house built into the caverns on the side of the mountains. As he smells the aroma of a hot meal, his path is left for comfort.

Leaving his powers behind is not noticed when leaving the mountain trail. Soon after, he finds himself at the steps.

Hearing his feet on the steps, Ezmarelda slips through a door and into the cavern. She then closes her eyes on this world and opens them to the heavenlies in silent prayer.

A knock is heard at the door and Zena goes to answer it while Nilda stirs the stew. Upon opening the door, Chaffie sees Claire sitting in a chair at the table as he enters before noticing Zena who bids him in, "Is that you, Chaffie?"

"You remember me."

"Looks like you've had a bad day."

"I was chased by a bear almost all the way here."

"Don't just stand there, come on in and tell us about it," Claire speaks out.

Nilda gives invitation while stirring the stew, "Perhaps you'll join us for breakfast?"


Reaching the ship, Sono calls out to the watch, "I need help!" He collapses on the beach.

The last thing he hears is the splash of the long-boat hitting the water 'til he regains consciousness while being settled in the bunk. He notices his head has been bandaged as he hears the first mate's voice, "What happened while you were in Dagog?"

Sono turns his head to the Captain who stands next to Oxer after looking over from Skip and says, "Please! I am on an urgent mission and must get to the other side of the river at once."

"Weigh anchor, Oxer. Skip, take the wheel and set course for the other side. Look for signs of a trail on the sure line once we get there and call me if you see one, I'll be here with Sono."

"Aye-aye, Captain!" says the crew and then they are off.

Captain Cantik asks, "What is this mission you are on?"

"That my people would fall back in line with eternity again from being disrupted by time."

"Can you say that in layman's terms?"

"I am going to help my people."

"Rest easy there, we'll have you across in no time."

Having left the village of Ostrog and bidding their farewells to an elated people, Prince Liam with the accompaniment of his wife and brother spent the rest of the day riding on. Through the pass of the mountains of Zantee, past the tall hills, and the Seeing Pools, they rode. Much ground was covered, riding across the desert while riding by night. They avoided the tribe of Bashna's community under the instruction of Nettle and Morris by passing through Roughco's camp instead with no little commotion. There was much celebration, a season of fellowship, and a time of refreshment while there. Then moving on, they finished traveling the forest.

Next, stopping at the village where the sand creatures became men again when the truth was tested, in catching up, it was learned that there was a dispute over a lack of food and water. With no solution in sight, Liam discussed the problem with them 'til a return to faith settled them. For in the heat of their dispute, he told them to pray and rely on the Lord for a solution, "If you trust and call upon The Great One, all will be worked out. Have prayer and meditations of song on your hearts with thanksgiving and your focus shall be restored. As in being summoned to go back to Dagog, I must continue on. So, wait for my return and Lord willing, I shall have an answer for you." After his final words, He promises to pray for them as well.

Now, just as he was directed by The Great One to go to the Dailey River with no way to cross, Prince Liam must wait for a peaceful resolution for them on this matter, too.


Chaffie politely places his spoon on the table. Nilda offers him another helping and he realizes that there is something very different about their manner. Having been refreshed, he comments, "Since when have you three become so kind… and what has happened to that other sister of yours, besides Katrina? Remember how she lost her powers in the end, for the good of us all?"

"Ezmarelda's on an errand right now. As for your thoughts, I must let you know that my ideas were the same as you at one time 'til realizing how alone I was. For I embraced the seductive light of condemnation to justify why I did not need to know the depth of a love that led to The Great One. As in leading me away from a beauty that was offered in place of what was light, evil gave me a deceptive and darkened mind by being dim in my vision at one time. For in my sight, I was left blind to not have sight when not realizing I was calling a sewer ditch a living life. With rotten stench, I called this evil good and fresh air foul, which could have been an eternal mistake if not for Prince Liam and Ashley."

With Chaffie's demons subdued by all their prayers, he is quick to respond as in the beginning of going through a door, "You've sparked my interest as by being slowed to the friction of conviction, which I had confused with condemnation; I'm found suddenly warm within my heart. So, I ask of you to tell me more."

"You speak of friction and warmth of heart. Well, beyond warmth of light, a fire burns brighter 'til beyond all the dimness where there is the brilliance of pure light, one that invites the Great One and Christ, by igniting us into the deepest love of a full life."

"Exiting all that is pleasing to my senses in dark, a sight has been granted to enter a new realm of light. How intriguing in my sight."

"Behind the presence of this light lay a person opposite of night. Would you like to meet this one whose brilliance opens up minds in a fullness of life with the greatness of The Great One in full depth of love which shines so bright?"

"I have just now received a revelation of light, which has burned away all dimness from me. For I have received salvation in my sight and know of love where once was drought."

A burst of gladness fills the room where in celebration all rejoice. Claire shares what is on her heart, "To understand the light of the one you've just embraced in love, there is a *Book of Life* that will explain it all."

Although he acts excited as a little child, it is really all a performance to cover up a secret that invites a fade of light within behind his eyes. For in his embarrassment, Chaffie doth not want to say what is unkind inside his mind, *"I cannot read!"*

He immediately becomes uneasy and further lies by excusing himself after placing the book upon the table, "I can't wait to read what it contains, but first I must relieve myself."

Once outside the door, he just keeps going 'til back on the trail. The foothold of darkness he's created within, leaves just enough room for all the dark spirits to gain a stronghold. He is reminded of his lust for greed and power and falls to the ground in a spiritually drunken stupor, convulsing as they enter back in.

Prince Liam and his companions are just arriving at the shore of the Dailey River when he sees the vessel draw close from across the river.

"Look, Liam. A ship!"

"I see it too, Edward."

Onboard the good ship, *Hope it Floats*, Sono notices Prince Liam and the others on shore.

Captain Cantik notices how the dwarf perks up and asks, "Are those friends of yours?"

Sono excitedly responds, "Friends… and oh, so much more."

"What do you mean by… so much more?"

"He is the one who has brought news of the Great One originally. He has not only set us free from the spell of a witch, but showed us the way to eternal life. He is the one who is son to the father of all who established the land of Calington so minds be free to embrace all light to know The Great One, who is the Christ!"

"Are you saying that if it were not for his family line, we would not have experienced the freedom of eternal life within our being?"

"Let me ask you a question."

Cantik looks on attentively at Sono…

"What happens to a butterfly that never frees itself of its cocoon?"

There is a moment of silence before receiving his response, "I get your meaning as I have tasted freedom after being bound!"

"Well, Prince Liam over there is one of the reasons you know of the Great One for that freedom."

"Liam. What a fine noble name. Perhaps you would introduce me?"

"You're coming ashore?"

"Yes, I would like to thank…"

Oxer calls out, "Captain, I'm getting a reading of three fathoms on the pole."

"Drop anchor and join me by the longboat, our passenger needs to make it to shore."

Sono smiles in disbelief. Not only is he on schedule, but he shall get to see Princes Liam and Edward, along with Ashley, once more.

Watching the longboat hit the water, Prince Edward turns to his brother and says, "Looks like we have some company, Liam."

"Thanks be to The Great One! Yes, we have a way to cross!"

"Isn't the dwarf with a bandage on his head Sono?"

Oxer rows in a little closer before Liam has better sight of the boat.

Prince Liam says to his wife, "You have good eyes, my dear."

Prince Edward gets down off of his horse, sits down on the beach, and starts taking off his boots. "Well, if I am going on a ship, at least my boots will be dry."

"What a good act of faith, my brother." Liam follows suit and takes off his boots. Ashley then doth the same. Liam turns to his horse and says while taking off its saddle, "I hope you are ready for a swim."

When the longboat reaches shore, Princes Liam and Edward are there to help them beach and bring the boat ashore.

An eager Captain motions to Sono for an introduction to Prince Liam who calls to the one with the bandage on his head, "Would that be you, Sono?"

He responds by saying, "It is you, my prince. I thought I recognized you from the boat. Oh! And this is Captain Cantik who got me here."

Cantik takes Liam's hand as he is helped out of the longboat and says, "Thank you, matey… and thank you for the freedom I have within my soul."

"No thanks is needed as everything is done in accordance with the timing of the Great One. Speaking of which, if you are in agreement, I would like passage for the three of us across the river, the horses can swim it."

"It would be my honor to take you across on the *Hope it Floats*."

"Ha! What a clever name," says Ashley who overhears.

"How did you come up with a name like that?" asks Prince Edward.

"Well, let's just say my other ship did not fare as well and it was a long swim back from the sea."

Prince Liam suggests, "I would like to hear more of your adventure after I ask a few questions of my own. Sono, how did you come to have a bandage on your head?"

"When I was walking back from Dagog, Chaffie attacked me."

"Chaffie is in Dagog already? Come forth, my brave dwarf." Liam lays his hands gently on his head and says, "In the name of The Great One, Jesus Christ, be healed." Sono's mouth opens wide and his eyes light with joy as Edward removes the bandage from his head. Captain Cantik and his crew look on in astonishment as Prince Liam inquires, "Tell me all of what you know."

# Across the River

The horses are swimming the river as the *Hope it Floats* sails not too far ahead. Captain Cantik just finished telling his tail of how he lost his first ship *Tierra* when Liam asks, "How large is the town you come from?"

"I would say about two square miles, give or take some feet or so. Why do you ask?"

"Is your town open to new people settling there?"

"You might say that."

"Do you have any ordinances for newcomers?"

"All newcomers are welcome. In fact, our whole town is open in all honesty."

"How is that?"

"Me and my crew are the only survivors of a plague that was once in our town."

"How long ago was the plague?"

"Easy now. It has been several years and the fact that Sono and the others are still alive, there is no more threat."

"Well then, I see you are the one I need to talk to. For as a sea captain, you are the high ranking official in the town, which would make you the mayor."

"I never thought of it this way before."

"Now, as the acting mayor, captain, how would you like some residents in your town?"

"Let me discuss it with the other occupants of the town." Captain Cantik cries out, "Mates!"

They look over from their ship duties and say together in acknowledgement, "Aye, captain."

"How would you like to have some permanent company in our town?"

Skip responds while steering at the helm, "Sounds good!" Oxer nods a big yes as he handles the mainsail.

"There you have it, Prince Liam. My first council meeting and the vote is yes."

"Splendid. Now if you'd be good enough to draw out a map, I know of those who would consider this an answer to prayer."

"Step into my cabin and I'll draw out for you where the town of Sedwick be."

The waves crash against the bow as Edward and Ashley watch the horses swim while looking over the side of the ship.

Skip, seeing Edward and Ashley watching them swim, calls out, "I bet you the gray finishes first."

Ashley calls back, "That all depends."

"On what?" asks Skip.

"On whether or not a wager is involved."

"Oh! Come on now, there's nothing wrong with having a little sport, is there?"

Ashley turns to her brother and says, "You tell him, Edward."

He nods and shouts out, "Not unless you've learned to love the truth of The Great One more!"

Skip buttons his lip and ponders for a moment as his captain walks out on deck. Prince Liam follows him out while tucking the map in an inner pocket.

Cantik calls Oxer, "Let loose on the sail and let's beat those horses in so Prince Liam and the others will be ready for them when they come in from their swim.

Oxer forwards the sail 'til the captain says, "Okay, take down the sail and prepare to drop anchor. Skip, take us in on the starboard side."

"Aye-aye, captain," is heard throughout the ship.

"Oxer, drop anchor, then the two of you meet me by the longboat."

"Aye-aye!"


Chaffie walks a good and even pace on the mountain trail, but a little more apprehensively after his encounter with the bear earlier on. Yet as he moves onward, thoughts of only how he'll succeed to the exclusion of all else gradually possess his mind.


Sono huffs and puffs, catching his breath while leaning on the stone dividing wall, the great forest is just ahead of him. He pauses for a moment of prayer until his peace returns along with his breath. Carried by The Great One, although he has a sense of urgency, his mind remains at rest while staying on Him. As he now travels into the forest at a brisk pace of certainty, his heart remains warm within.

With horses mounted, Prince Liam gives final instruction to Captain Cantik, "We should be back in a few days, but as to not be presumptuous if no word is heard within two weeks, take the extra copy of where Sedwick is located and deliver it as we discussed while in the cabin."

"Aye-aye!"

After turning his horse, Prince Liam rides between Ashley's and Edward's and leads them on into a gallup. The beach is quick to leave their sight as they cover much ground at a rapid pace. After an hour's worth of hard riding, they go into a trot 'til coming to a pool of water where they rest their animals. While giving them a hearty drink, Edward suggests, "By the looks of the sun, we should reach Claire and her sisters at around five o'clock."

"Sounds about right," says Liam.

Ashley looks on and silently prays.

Morris and Nettle ride the front of the wagon together while Manfried and Gyus ride in the back. While entering the monastery, Morris pulls back on the reigns and brings them to a stop. Nettle looks over to Morris and says, "I do not know what to tell anyone."

"A picture says a thousand words and yet I am left speechless, too," says Morris.

Overhearing their conversation, Manfried suggests, "Perhaps the two of you should come with us when giving a report to Bartholomew as he is one who has great wisdom."

"I will come," says the two dwarfs."

Gyus then states, "After you water and put up the horse, I believe we will be in the Lord's timing."

Within the forest, Sono realizes that he is approaching the village. So, about a mile out of camp, he veers from the main trail and disappears from sight. Reappearing without his pack and hood up, he hopes to go unnoticed among his tribe. While walking, a strategy now comes to mind on how to get Billy away from his house. Then with a little further prayer, he requests just how he is supposed to get Ella Elf to drink the serum, which will change her back into being Bella, the dwarf.

Knocking on the door to the Monsignor's office, Bartholomew bids entrance to Manfried. When the door opens, Gyus and the dwarfs follow in right behind him.

After looking up from the desk, Bartholomew asks, "How did everything go at the village, Manfried?"

"Miraculous!"

"I take it that Prince Liam received the message of invitation then?"

Gyus volunteers, "Yes, he was… And The Great One was upon him as One and the same, for he was used to restore a boy mauled by wild dogs and raise him from the dead. I have never seen anything like it."

"What about you two, Morris and Nettle? What do you have to say?"

Morris responds, "I do not know what to say."

"Humility is always a good place to start."

"How about you, Nettle?"

He raises his hand and shrugs, "I don't know either."

"Let me share what is on my heart concerning you both. Blessed are those who have seen and blessed are those who have not seen."

Nettle interrupts, "But we have now seen!"

Morris comments as well, "Now that we have seen, things feel different and I do not know why."

Bartholomew responds to their troubled hearts, "Let not your hearts be troubled nor let them be afraid. So let it be known, you shall never walk alone."

"But how are we to share what we've experienced?"

"Let all your boasting be in the Lord. Your countenances are alighted with joy and let this be a first boast. Then if people ask why, just plainly tell them and finish the boast as this will be a testimony that is confirmed by your actions."

Nettle then asks, "So, we are not to give proclamations of what has happened before our very eyes then?"

"Not unless asked or it comes up in conversation."

"I do not understand," says Morris.

Bartholomew ponders to himself for a moment before he answers, "Have you ever gone fishing?"

"Yes."

"I have, too," says Nettle.

"Can you catch a fish by jumping in the water with a splash to grab one?"

They answer, "No."

"Well, pretend you are the bait as what you offer in accordance with the actions behind your words will determine if you are going to satisfy your hunger for truth or starve. For according to the *Book of Life*, a laborer is worthy of their hire. So, remember to remain in The Great One's timing by keeping your peace and you shall always reap His King's reward."

The two look on and joyfully nod.

# Chaffie's Stand

Sono goes unnoticed among his tribe as he walks with his hood up. He then moves towards the outer perimeter of the forest where the outhouses are. Then when no one is looking, he darts off to the side out of sight where he is able to keep a comfortable eye on Billy's place. Looking through the trees and up into the sky, it is figured to be near five at eve. Sono knows that when Billy goes to supper, he will have an ample chance to get into the house.

After watching Billy leave the house, Sono starts for the door. Passing the central fire pit along the way, he realizes he has a lot of wood to gather before the fire can be lit. He knocks on the door to Billy's cabin and receives no answer before letting himself in. Upon entry, he sees Ella Elf sipping some brew from a tea set.

Ella becomes indignant as she proclaims, "How dare you enter my chambers unannounced!"

Sono then speaks out against her darkness, "Bella… Bella, I know it is you who are there."

She suddenly freezes at the mention of her real name as from beneath her darkness, a pin prick of true light has acknowledged who she really is. "How do you know me?"

Sono says her name again and adds instruction as he holds out the vial that contains the serum from the righteous tree, which looks like a praying man from a distance. "Bella!" On seeing her response to hearing her name, he realizes that light is invading her darkness, "Bella! Bella!" On saying her name the third time, she becomes unfrozen. "Drink this down," Sono says while handing her the vial. Bella doth so at once.

Suddenly, there is a poof of green smoke and standing before him now is Bella the dwarf, Basha's wife.

He takes her by the hand and announces, "Come on, we have some wood to gather and a fire to light.

Prince Liam and the others dismount their horses and find their way 'til their leader's hand knocks upon the door.

Claire rises from prayer with her sisters and opens the door, "Oh! You are a sight for sore eyes and an answer to prayer. For you have come at a crucial time. Yet, do not even stop. Get on your horses and ride to the mountains for a battle is about to take place between Chaffie and the priests."

Prince Liam instructs, "Ashley, remain here with your mother and aunts and pray for us unceasingly as this will be our third cord, which cannot easily be broken. For you are my wife!"

Claire shouts after them, "Chaffie can be persuaded back from out of all the darkness which now holds him, Prince Liam." He waves before they pull their horses from the water trough after mounting up. Soon, they disappear from sight towards the mountains.

Chaffie is on foot and rapidly nears the prayer trap on the ground which has been claimed in the name of The Great One as the well concealed Monsignor and I watch him approach.

A fire roars as the darkness of night falls in the great forest which makes the light from its flame visible to everyone leaving the dining area and the crowd of onlookers who follow along.

Bashna steps out from the crowd and demands the dwarf who has his hood up, "What is the meaning of this? Who has told you to light the central flame to eternity?

Sono calls out, "Bella, it is time!"

She steps out from behind the flame and Basna is taken aback as is everyone else.

Bashna speaks out in a sense of wonderment, "Bella, is it really you?"

"If you do not wish to lose me again, you must do as I say."

"I do not understand."

Bella says to Bashna, "It is either me or the stone."

All at once, everyone holds their personal stone in the air up towards the sky.

Sono realizes in his mind, *This must be the sign!*

Chaffie is almost out of the prayer zone when Bolo the gnome gets his attention. Within the shadow of a large stone, he calls out, "You do not have to do this!"

The dwarf warlock stops and questions, "Who said that?"

The monsignor and I suddenly come out from our place of concealment. While walking towards Chaffie, I trip over a rock and fall forward, spilling out my long-knife from my pack before the dwarf.

Becoming suddenly paranoid, Chaffie shouts, "You have come to kill me, assassins!" After picking up the knife, the dwarf advances to run me through and says, "I knew you priests were liars."

The Monsignor calls to him, "If we're liars, then run me through first."

"It doth not matter who gets it." All at once, I dive in front of the Monsignor as Chaffie lunges forward.


Sono yells, "For the love of your life, throw your stone into the fire, Bashna, and behold your bride again."

Without hesitation, Bashna throws his stone into the fire. As it explodes, it releases the reality of a greater love than what this gem had to offer. For the picture of greater love permeates the air with a stronger embrace as God's love is remembered.

All the other stones begin to be hurled at the flame as well.

I look down and notice my knife sticking through me as I have been run through by Chaffie who withdraws my blade from me in the moonlight. While collapsing to the ground, I hear the sound of clippity-clop hoofbeats approaching.

The blade is withdrawn from me and I'm now found half on the ground with my head on the Monsignor's lap.

Chaffie turns as Princes Liam and Edward dismount from their horses. He shouts after them, "I've been waiting for you, Prince Liam," who is drawing his sword. "Even with your brother and a hundred men, you could not withstand the power of my masterstone."

Taking out the bright and shining green gemstone while holding it in the palm of his hand, it suddenly dims 'til turning black as coal. "Sono, he must have gone to Bashna! I never should have let him get by!"

"Chaffie, don't end up like your mentor Katrina. For Claire has told me that you have tasted of the Great One's Spirit."

Remaining defiant, he gives his response, "God means nothing to me now!"

"Watch what you now hold in your heart and hand, for it might be there without your full permission. Look carefully and you will see that the battle is really of a spiritual nature. They seduce you to believe that you really want more than what you have. So, do not let these dragons that live within keep you numb in what you have. For what lives in the dark, which even now captures the thoughts inside your mind, needs to be rebuked by God. Give yourself permission to let The Great One's hug embrace you from within, then you'll experience His love inside yourself by the use of your own arms in the power of His revelations. He shall hold you from what you remember of His first touch of love as even now He can set you free. Do not deny the discomforts of what is keeping you irritable and restless. For your spirits want a lust of power to have you drunk in blurry eyes. No changes will happen as long as you believe that you can control your need for something more."

The little warlock vehemently speaks out, "Tell yourself a lie 'til all be true, but as for me, no way."

"Life is not about having power, nor living it alone. Live instead to just be alive and know The Great One's simplicities of reward of joy."

Edward becomes involved, "Is God not greater than all your miseries? For what you do not see or know is killing you even now."

Chaffie says angrily, "Do not play with me, boy!"

Edward states plainly, "No games here as you need a defense that will seal you with protection from within or you will continue to have unkind consequences."

I next hear Liam say, "What did Katrina promise you? Power over others because you were shorter than them? Stop and be compliant or you shall always know the misery of a defiance that knows no love. For without full understanding, you will never know how to rely upon the God of joy for more than a short season, which shall torment you in the end. You know this and yet you practice it anyway, a ritual that leaves you in the dark to not comprehend why you reach for what destroys. Is this what you want?"

"My spirits serve me just fine."

"Watch the thoughts inside your mind. For if they do not look like the character of love, they aren't. I would even say you look to escape waves of trouble by seeking solutions that are beyond your understanding. This is why I make every effort to subject myself to only seeing love 'til the Great One captivates me with a peace which guards both my heart and mind.

Now look over there and tell me what you see?" He points to me bleeding to death in the Monsignor's lap.

"I see two men, one of which is dying," says Chaffie.

"Why is that man dying?"

"Because he needlessly threw himself in front of another man."

"Now you are beginning to see. For no greater love doth one have than he lay down his life for a friend."

"Love is blind!"

"No, love has sight, for it lives forever. Only what blinds from seeing this has no love as these spirits are evil."

"This love is not in me and I'm not evil."

"Look at your actions and see if there is something deeper that is lacking within. For if you let love embrace with a hug that will hold, you shall know it more deeply than what you now have inside your soul.

The Great One and Christ wants this glory for you. Then when more glory comes, you shall know that you're in the light of His hand. For the knowledge of God's mercy brightens to give more of Himself, which is a free gift for you.

"This is a love that I could appreciate more than what I had with the Monsignor's sisters than before, to embrace myself with His deep heart even more."

"Where you have ignored God before has led to a darkness that did not allow you to see your actions as you reached for a power which was destroyed. In the past, I was guilty of the same 'til I counted my blessing to know God more than my troubles at hand and now my life's become a treasure that I have no desire to give away."

"Now I see my connection with The Great One has been my problem and not my troubles at hand. For by my actions, I danced with death without the knowledge of His life in my heart."

"If you are willing, we can train you to see the depth of the love of Christ before any desire or urge that would cause you to reach for something other than God's pure hand of life."

"But I am frustrated as I cannot read the *Book of Life* to know The Great One more."

"Do not let this trouble you, but look to the bridegroom who is The Christ and you will know that by his blood sacrifice, He has prepared Himself for you. So, be adorned to become his bride by action and word with heavenly deeds that will make you one as in marriage to the holy one of light that darkness will not overtake your hand again."

"What must I do to live the words which I cannot read as I am ready to be his bride?"

"Your willing heart is a first thread and know that because it belongs to Him, He will clothe you in all of righteousness. For when He was immersed in water Himself as Great One and Lord as our example, He said, 'Let us fulfill what is right.'"

Throwing down the longknife, Chaffie says, "I want to commit as our Great One and Christ did. I see a pool of water. What is there to prevent me from being baptized?"

"Look there. Your brother is in need of tending to first."

"Oh my! He is my brother now. I cannot bear what I have done. Lord, I call to You. Do not let him die."

"You bear another thread as it is the Spirit of truth which crafts us into all holiness with His guiding finger. For He points our hearts in the right direction where truth be found in place of lies. Now as your love has grown with desires for him to live and not die, I am moved by deeper love to lay my hands which belong to the Lord's on his wound even while they are yet mine."

I watch as prince Liam comes over with Chaffie standing by His side and lays his warm hands on my wound. The heat from his hands become warmer than my own blood and then I can tell that I have been touched by love. When he takes his hands away, I feel my strength return and say, "Come on, let's get you baptized and adorned for The Christ, your bridegroom. Now receive the completion of His resurrection seed in heavenly places while on earth as His bride."

Chaffie looks over and points, "That knife on the ground, I know I put it right through you!"

Prince Liam states, "The Great One is the God of new beginnings."

"Yes, I am ready for this insurgence of new life that I may grow to know Him even more this day."

I rise and take Chaffie by the hand then bury him into the oneness of the nearby pool of water to fulfill the word of God, "In the name of the Father, Son, and Holy Spirit, I baptize you anew into the kingdom of heaven, receive now the adorning of eternal life.

Upon him coming up out of the water, Princes Liam and Edward take extra blankets and wrap them around him as there is a chill in the night air.

Prince Liam then informs Chaffie, "All of creations sings glory to the Creator. Learn the song of each and every part of it and your relationship with Him shall grow very strong. For cultivating gratitude within all He offers will allow your relationship to flourish with Him in every detail of your life 'til you are sealed from looking away from being alive.

Now the Monsignor has prepared a thanksgiving meal that the song of all creation points to in its entirety, which shall give you the full picture of what you will learn to comprehend over time. For while you're taught to read from the *Book of Life*, study the nature of all things so you can better focus on what we call the Eucharist. We are granted flesh and blood from the body of the seed of the resurrection from The Christ to impregnate us, the bride, to experience eternal life. You will not always know how growth happens in the grace and knowledge of The Great One, but it will be easy to understand that you are changing inside your soul while becoming whole."

The newly born again dwarf says, "I will observe nature everyday 'til the Creator of it speaks to me of something more concerning Him."

Liam responds, "Then your life will flourish, becoming rich and full."

The Monsignor has the elements ready at the altar of the marriage supper of the lamb's table. We walk over and I inform Chaffie that since he has become a part of the church as bride through baptism, he is ready to meet the bridegroom in a new covenant marriage to which the *Book of Life* refers.

# Journeying Home
# by Way of the Gnomes

**B**ack in my pocket, Bolo takes in the night air as I mount the horse behind Prince Edward. Our gnome friend says, "Hey, easy there. We still have Puppco to contend with back at the village."

"What village, Marcus… and just who would Puppco be?" asks the prince.

"Oh, you're talking about what my little talkative friend is saying, not me."

"Little friend?"

"Let me introduce you two. For within all the commotion, I haven't had a chance."

Edward turns his head and looks over his shoulder, "I don't see anyone."

"No, look here!" Placing my hand by my pocket, Bolo steps into it and then I present him to Prince Edward.

"Why, he's even shorter than a dwarf!"

The gnome reacts by saying, "Enough sas, man. Now are you coming to help free my friend?"

"The first I've heard of it. What friend?"

I then give an account for Bolo, "I know he's a bit straightforward…"

"No matter, I like it when someone gets straight to the point. Did you ever notice how some people get around to telling you what's on their mind?

Now, what has happened to your friend that has you so uneasy?"

"He has been taken captive by dragon spirits."

"Sounds serious." He then calls to his brother and the Monsignor who rides from behind him along with Chaffie who is looking on attentively, "Liam, there is someone among us who is in need of our help that I believe you should meet."

"I heard everything as all was carried by the wind," says Liam.

"As did I," acknowledges Chaffie.

"Desperation can often drive one. This is why it is better to keep your peace before you open your mouth."

"I can attest to that as I can see how everyone who is at peace finds acceptance with God first before he finds it with others. For praying to Him is the key that opens the door for The Spirit of light to calm the dragons of the dark, just as mercy triumphs over judgment."

"A lot of truth in what you said. I can see how you've grown in your relationship with the great One already. Now, I feel any further talk should be done back at the Monsignor's sisters' house. For you never know which way the winds are blowing."

"The Monsignor then adds, "Well spoken, Prince Liam." We then begin journeying for the shelter of his sisters' dwellings with the light of the moon.

Back at the cabin adjoined to the caverns, some strategizing is going on, "I have thought this through while on our ride over. Chaffie, you are to remain here and receive instruction from the Monsignor's sisters and learn some more ways of meditating on creation to better understand the Creator."

"I thought I was going with you to cast evil spirits out of the gnome," says the dwarf.

"You are still very sensitive and having just crossed over to the light would leave you tender to the belch of these foul spirits. For when being cast out, they would seek you first."

He responds with a very humbling, "I understand."

"Why do you understand?" asks Claire.

"I no longer have to play a role or guess at life as I have found the stability of eternal life. For now I am married to The Great One himself who steadies me to know just who I am."

"That's good for a start. I believe we can work together. I am in agreement, Prince Liam. We shall train him like we have done with the others."

Prince Liam turns to his brother while removing the map that shows where the town of Sedwick is located.

"I understand that I am not to come either," says Edward.

"It's not that you aren't able to come. It's just…"

"This is more important. I understand, Liam." He takes the map and starts for the door.

"Wait! For I am going to come with you," says the Monsignor who hugs his sisters goodbye after kissing his niece, Ashley, on the cheek. "For there can still be other spirits in this land of enchantment."

"My thoughts exactly," says Prince Liam.

Prince Liam, Ashley, and I look to each other before he speaks again, "A threefold cord cannot easily be broken. We three shall travel with Bolo, who will direct us through Dagog to the village. Chaffie, your first assignment will be to pray for our safety for three days. Claire, you and your sisters do the same and by that time this whole ordeal should be over with.

Now, it be best if we all got some rest before heading out on the morrow. This way, we shall all have our wits about us and be able to move out in The Great One's timing of peace."

I then suggest, "There is another way to cross the river I know of on our return trip."

"For some reason, I am to go to Sedwick… Edward, tell Captain Cantik that he should return for us and wait after he has taken you across."

"Gotcha!"

The rest of us settle down for a period of rest. All peace has now been restored for us to function as a single body of believers early on at morn.

On the road, the sky turns from twilight to sunrise at dawn as Prince Edward and the Monsignor share riding the horse back down through the mountains of Dagog towards the river.

Prince Edward shares what is on his heart to the Monsignor as he questions, "Do you really believe my slip of tongue could release a greater evil than what Chaffie was trying to accomplish?"

"Anything is possible in the mountains of Dagog, but keep in mind, The Christ has overcome the world."

Prince Liam, Ashley, and I travel afoot as the terrain is too rocky for horse. At first, the prince offers to carry the gnome that he could lead us on, yet Bolo draws a line and says, "Please do not be offended, but I would rather travel with my old friend Marcus."

"No offense taken as there is nothing like the company of an old friend. We will still get there."

"I see that you retain the spirit of wisdom by your words, for they are still the same as when you spoke to Chaffie."

"These words are not mine, Bolo. This is how I know the dragon spirit that holds your friend will be defeated. Greater is He that is in me than he that is in the world."

We walk through many twisting narrow turns as directed by Bolo whom I carry. Prince Liam and his wife follow me right behind. I can tell that the passageways we walk would have been too narrow for horse. Our source of sunlight shines intermittently through the crevices of rock formations in which we pass.

Bolo calls to Prince Liam, "I believe it would be wise for you to know the name of my friend that you can call to him in his darkness while guiding him towards light.

"And what would his exact name be?"

"His name is Puppco."

"It seems you know a great deal about spiritual principles, Bolo. So, why did you not cast them out?"

"My knowledge is from being bold in selfish pride and not from having words from the *Book of Life* alive inside me like you."

"I shall have to remedy this situation by explaining to you what the voices of these dragon spirits really are. So that you, as their leader, may disarm them of their power before disbanding them. To start off, can you describe the character of The Great One for me?"

"Well, He is kind, gentle, and compassionate with love."

"Did you yourself not just exhibit these qualities of mercy by seeking help for your friend?"

Bolo becomes silent and listens while they walk the rocks. He finally answers him, "You humble me with your words."

Prince Liam speaks to his new attitude, "There have been times in my own life that I have needed humbling from my own selfish pride, too. Once we recognize this, Bolo, we are ready to receive the Lord's confidence with lives that center around Him.

Abasing is a must for us to abound as in humbling ourselves in the sight of the Lord, He will lift us up. Higher and higher shall He lift us when we exalt Him 'til entering into a brightness that is so brilliant that darkness itself shall fade.

The redeemed of the Lord can say, I will return and come with singing unto the heights of The Great One Himself. Light shines on the heads of untold smiles from a peace that rests within any lives which truly know Him with an everlasting joy which shall make itself manifest as crowns of life placed within them.

Yes! You shall obtain great mercy and voices of morning and sorrow shall flee away. Selfish pride from your confidence that has been a problem for you will be replaced by God's confidence from knowing to call upon His face. No dragon spirit can stand against the greater attitude of His bonding love from little gratitudes, which are setting you into position to hold big blessings. His zeal will find you consumed to lift you up from out of any dark pit. He shall then reign in the midst of you forever and ever for as long as your heart allows Him. So, rest comfortably in His place and He will remain on a throne of unity inside to ignite your life continually.

As you recognize the restraints of His love, you will know what the voice of love is in the face of other spirits that will try to break this love. This is important for you to not only know but be unified with as you are in a covenant marriage with God by His Spirit with a bond that dragons will try and break. Now as a part of Him, He shall slay any dragon that would try to attach itself to your soul as you will be able to tell Him everything that is not of love.

If you doubt what I say, then they are at work on you already." By the light that shines in my eyes, I notice that the sun has moved within the sky.

Bolo answers, "I have no doubt about it."

"Good, then you are now ready to learn how to do battle with the dragon of pride within yourself first so that you will be ready to cast them out of others. For with spirits in your land, they will attack others and as their leader, you must know what to do about it."

"But I am not ready to do such a thing."

"Humility is always a good place to start as it will be recognized that you need a power greater than yourself to call upon to defeat any spirits that try to destroy. So, know this well: be bold in prayer. For God will protect His child that cries out as it is His desire to wipe away all their tears."

"What must I do? I am ready by faith to know of His words by hearing them through you."

"You know that love is gentle, patient, and kind. So, now let us look at what would try to distract this from your mind from what I've learned by The Great One's Spirit.

A dragon will try to intimidate you from believing that there's a God of creation capable of love. It doth not want you to know how precious you are to Him or that He is capable of loving others in the same way which are different from you. Although He establishes boundaries on how to love each other best, there's a blindness that dims minds. When people do not listen and violate themselves or others, He gets the blame while thoughts are dark. This is the first voice of a dragon which is well concealed in what they invite as they're all the same when they try and drain.

A second voice will try to attack you from influences by spirits that surround. Getting you to draw from anger in place of love with the purpose of bringing division from within is its ploy. So, keep your faith within this place and remember what has been built upon your first love with Him. For if you so choose to call on the God of love instead of your anger, He will protect you in His bond and defeat any dragon spirit here. It will also defeat the dragon in the other person while embracing the better choice of the kingdom of peace which calms all down. For in knowing the deeper, more satisfying truth of peace by choice, the darkness yields to The Great One's Spirit of light by the fonder affection to embrace freedom in life.

So, when the dragon breathes fire at you with lies telling you you're not worthwhile inside, look to the truth of the Lord and know the value of His love instead. Be filled with life in place of stinging death and you will light with life by the Christ living within you when the dragon comes to shake. For with the self esteem of God's love inside, the dragon will be shaken back into the abyss instead of taking you by surprise."

We stop for a drink of water on a ledge that takes in a view of where we can see everything below. I now recognize some familiar terrain off in the distance and comment, "Look there to the left, just northeast of those rocks. That mist you see rising must be from the waterfall where the Dailey River nears its end."

"…It is by the bog, I can tell from the whiff of it," says Prince Liam.

Further up the river, the Monsignor and Prince Edward arrive at the beach on his horse, which begins to kick up the sand from beneath its hooves by the sudden change of ground.

Skip cries out, "Captain, there is a horse on the beach with riders."

"Can you tell who it is yet?"

"I see Prince Edward's brown horse and from the size of his passenger, the Monsignor is with him."

"Oxer, make ready the longboat. Skip, place a water barrel on the hoist, we'll take on fresh drinking water before we cross."

"Aye-aye, captain!"

Coming in from prayer, Ezmarelda closes the door at the rear of the cabin on the caverns. She goes over to Claire and whispers in her ear.

The eldest sister responds, "I will go as I know your visions be true."

She then turns to her other sisters as Claire goes outside, "It is time for us to pray as the others are a stones throw away from their destination."

Approaching the community of gnomes, we are met with warm greetings. "Look, Marcus has returned with Bolo and they have company with them," is heard as we enter their village.

Bolo asks the keeper of the records from the council, "What has happened since I have been away?'

He then gives his report, "Puppco has taken over a quadrant in the third district. He roams the streets and finds no rest as he howls at the wind at night."

Prince Liam interjects, "Where is he in the quadrant now?"

The keeper of records answers, "We do not know as all of us now keep our distance."

"Bolo, come with me. Ashley and Marcus, start praying for protection that light will prevail over darkness and love over hate."

"I do not know if I should come with you, Prince Liam, I might get in the way."

"Be encouraged, Bolo. For in discovering what you do not like about yourself in the light of truth today shall not destroy you on the morrow. So, if you remain humble before God after asking Him to remove any dark spirit, you shall always walk in His freedom."

Bolo looks at the prince for a long pause before answering, "I am short tempered just beneath the shallows of my flesh and do not like it."

"That is a spirit of anger which needs to be removed. Now that it has been identified in the light, it shall not be able to get back in if you make a request of The Great One and Christ. Ask in the name of Jesus according to His Character as Christ, then this dragon shall be removed and no longer return to enter back in. You shall not remain helpless in its face. Be in song now and it will remain gone to no longer toss you as the sea. So, keep your eyes on the calm of love in anger's face and you'll be kept by God's embrace. Do this now and know that this is a preparation to meet with the dragons that hold Puppco."

"I will not be anxious as before, but find His peace instead. Then finding His ground, I shall remain sound by standing in His greater presence. In the name of the Lord and Great One, Jesus Christ, foul spirit of anger be gone and do not return again."

I look up from prayer to notice a smile break forth on Bolo's face.

My new mentor, Prince Liam, speaks from his position of light, "The Blood of Christ by the power of the New Covenant in your veins has given you a full resurrection authority. For you are an ambassador to Jesus, The King."

"I am ready!" says Bolo.

"As long as you remain at peace, you are. For as knowledge puffs up, love edifies. You shall be protected from a prideful fall."

My mentor catches my eyes looking on and says, "Remember to pray and do not look away, for spirits always are on the prowl to distract you from a heart of love throughout the day."

I next bond my heart to the King of Love and hear footsteps as Prince Liam and Bolo head out to do battle against Puppco's dragons which have his mind. The thought comes to me and straightway attacks my mind, *"Puppco knows me! Perhaps this would aid in bringing him back."*

Having arrived on the beach at the other side of the Dailey River, Prince Edward finishes cinching his saddle to the wet underbelly of his horse while the Monsignor looks on.

The longboat is already on route back to the ship and when seeing this, he calls out, "Do not forget to pray for us all, Captain Cantick, as they are very important for the success of all our missions." The prince's hand is then extended before his face, which The Monsignor takes as he is helped onto the horse behind Edward.

"Take hold of my hand and we'll be off. Next stop, the village at Old Winnies Field."

"Let us hope we are on time to prevent any war."

"My Monsignor, you of all people should know that everything is done in the Great One's timing."

"Yes. I trust that there will be peace. Let it be so, my Great One. Let us arrive in the timing of Your good pleasure."

Under the guidance of Prince Edward, the horse takes off and enters the fields as they start on their way.

# Battle in the Quadrant
## Before Returning

**R**apidly passing by the first two districts from the outskirts of the village of the tiny gnome dwellings, due to their size, Prince Liam swiftly arrives at the quadrant with Bolo in his shirt pocket.

A problem immediately becomes apparent as only Bolo is small enough to enter their community alone without doing damage to his village.

Prince Liam is quick to ask Bolo, "Where is Puppco's dwelling?"

"Marcus gave him a large teasack to live in on his last visit. Find it and perhaps you will find him."

While Liam scouts around the eighth of a mile large quadrant, Bolo comments on how the village has prospered and grown since he's been away. "I believe I see the teasack," says the prince.

"Can you reach it with your hand?"

"No, it is well beyond my reach. I could lower you on the end of my sword to save you some time, then you would only have four more lengths to walk. It is a straight path, so you should not have any trouble finding it on your left.

Remember, the demons will lie to you with confusing thoughts, but do not second guess the love that holds you deeper than all else." While drawing his sword, Prince Liam says, "I will be with you in Spirit by prayer. Here, sit on the flat end of my sword and I will lower you in the right direction."

Bolo humbly states, "Liam, if you pray for me, I am sure all will go well." He climbs on the flat of the blade and sits down to maintain his balance.

The prince extends the sword while saying, "All will go well because The Great One is in control."

The blade touches the ground and Bolo slides off and starts on his way.

Voices seem to call out as he walks through the center of the village while passing many huts where at any moment, Puppco can attack him. Yet, fear knows no name in the eyes of Bolo as he looks to a love which gives him a joyful mind while he rests on the focus of peace from the kingdom of The Great One. When walking, he notices the position of the sun. A thought now attacks him about how it will be dark soon. No matter, it will not make a difference what has his mind as *"Dark and light are alike to The Great one."* For he now has a new eternal perspective.

All at once, he hears a voice shriek out from a shadowy corner, "Why seek you the living among the dead?"

*"That's a twist of verse if I ever heard it,"* Bolo ponders to himself.

Entering into the center of the street, twenty steps before him, stands Puppco. "Boo hoo hoo! You're living on the surface of a pond of shallow tears and what lies beneath them shall eat you! So, go home to the comforts of your home or I'll rip your ugly head off!"

Bolo looks to the Great One's love and he is not moved by the spirit of fear. It doth not breach the focus of his bond to the Lord and he maintains Him as his armor. Yet, Puppco shouts to intimidate him more, "I am god! Bow down and worship me and I'll let you live, you foolish gnome who believes you are wise."

A brown horse appears with two riders traveling towards the village of Old Winnies Field. They are seen by the one who keeps watch at the entrance to the village on the field. As they draw nearer, an elder is summoned who recognizes Prince Edward first and then realizes that the one riding with him is the Monsignor whom he has not seen since times past.

The elder's thoughts escape his mouth, "My good Monsignor, it has been a long time since you've passed this way. Yet, by what route did you arrive as you were not with Prince Edward and the others when they passed before?"

The Prince interjects, "Perhaps this note and map of a new location, which The Great One has provided to relieve your overcrowding, will explain all."

A look of astonishment meets his eyes and realizing fully what has been said, he shouts to the rest of the villagers, "Prince Liam has kept his word!"

The other villagers look over from what they're doing. "There shall be peace. For our overcrowding problem has come to an end!"

"Yes, it is true," says the Monsignor. Though, there is something more pressing right now as Prince Liam needs our prayers, for he is casting out demons from a gnome named Puppco. So, pray for them both!"

Everyone takes a knee and turns towards The Great One in prayer.


"Enter through the narrow gate; for the gate is wide and the road broad that leads to destruction, and those who enter through it are many." After Bolo speaks a verse of truth from the *Book of Life,* the demons shriek with loud screams.

He speaks again, "How narrow the gate and constricted the road that leads to life." Puppco drops to the ground and appears as though he is dead as Bolo walks over. Remaining unmoved and at rest in the Spirit of The Great One while looking down over him, his eyes suddenly open. "Puppco, be at peace and your uneasiness will end. Take my hand

and let us go see Marcus, he has come a long way to share more of The Great One's love."

"Marcus is here?" He lets out half a smile before his eyes turn black. "Who is this Captain Cantik who prays? No, you cannot have him. He belongs to us!" The demon shouts.

"Those who find eternal life are few as the blood of Christ now cries out from me in rebuke of you. Foul spirits be gone in Jesus name as His blood flows from being His offspring in my veins. The truth of His joy doth light my soul. Come and embrace me, Puppco, and be made whole within your soul." He starts to shake in convulsions until he floats off the ground. Bolo runs over and falls on him, "Be at peace now, Puppco, and do not be driven from within. Quiet your mind with stillness inside, for you are in the presence of the Almighty Messiah by the pure blood of the eternal seed of Him."

The person of truth who indwells Bolo with His presence presses out Puppco's darkness by the purity of His resurrection light and forces him back down to the ground by his sacrificial weight of sheer love. For no greater love doth one have that he lays down his life for a friend. Bolo then proclaims, "You have no power over him. Embrace me, Puppco, and do not believe the darkness of any dragon lies. For the fall you had inside the cave in inadequacy made you adequate as we are helpless, even from being embraced by what appears to be your pride."

Prince Liam sprinkles Holy Water on his drawn sword from a cordial he has in another pocket. Puppco lets out a final scream before embracing Bolo back to receive the truth of The Great One's love. Then from out of the essence of his being while opening his mouth, he lets a darkness that takes the form of a large dragon with a grand release 'til out. It charges towards Liam who raises his sword and smites the beast in holy righteousness. Setting it ablaze with glory light, it heads for the cave and burns in the air 'til gone before it can make it there.

Bolo and Puppco weep from the joy of freedom as they're alive with the fullness of life. Rising off his friend, he extends his hand and helps a smiling Puppco up to his feet.

A release of joy is then felt by Marcus and Ashley as eve turns to gladness of light within the night. From the cabin of Claire and her sisters to Captain Cantik's cabin on the *Hope it Floats* and everywhere, all burdens are lifted 'til there is no more despair.

Bolo stands before Prince Liam and makes an introduction, "This thorn to our flesh who has now added gems in our crowns of life is Puppco."

"Pleased to make your acquaintance." Extending his hand downward, the prince touches his fingertips to the palm of his hand and shakes. He then raises them, lifting them up in his palm where they step off into his left shirt pocket. Looking over to them, Prince Liam suggests, "Come on, let's go and join the others by the fire over there."

Puppco says to Prince Liam while he walks, "It is good to be riding high again..."

Bolo replies in response, "...Yes. When out from the darkness of any valley, we are always high on the love of life while in the doorway of light.

Stepping into the light of the camp, Ashley questions Liam with a smile, "All went well?"

"Yes, all is well."

He next turns to me while extending his hand and says, "I believe you have an old friend here who wants to say hello."

"Marcus, you are a welcome sight."

"As are you, Puppco."

Ashley interjects while leaning forward, "Well, Puppco, I am glad to make your acquaintance." She next questions her husband, "Liam, are we to go back for our horses?"

He answers while putting down the gnomes, "I feel led for us to return another way."

I volunteer, "I know a path which goes beneath a waterfall that will allow us to pass to the otherside of the river."

"No, Marcus. We are to walk up the beach to the *Hope it Floats*. This is the direction we are to take. It'd be best if we all got some sleep as we all have a long journey ahead of us on the morrow."

Prince Liam finds a comfortable place and leans with his back against a large slanted rock. Ashley follows and snuggles up next to him. I stretch and lay on the ground. Growing concerned, I ask, "What will we do for supply when we get to the other side of the river?"

The prince answers, "The Lord will supply."

"I should have known better."

# Meeting Beyond the beach

Splashes of sunlight dart across my eyes as it shines through the trees. Awaking, I look over and see that an altar has been laid out by someone with the proper elements in place.

Without question, I rise and become the bridegroom's hand and breaking the bread, I say, "This is My body which is given for you. Do this in remembrance of Me. This cup which is poured out for you is the new covenant in My blood. Do this as often as you drink it in remembrance of Me."

All at once, I am given a vision of the blood of Jesus dripping from the cross and into the elements of the celebratory bread and wine of thanksgiving, "As often as you eat this bread and drink this cup, you proclaim the death of the Lord until He comes." I then add the drop of water into the cup, signifying the glory hour of Jesus turning water into wine that started His ministry. Now it is us and The Great One being united with Him in baptism through the acquiescence of the firmament.

Feeding the church, His bride, from before the altar, I watch as everyone from the village of gnomes receives a portion of the bread of thanksgiving and become satisfied with eternal life. Ashley administers the water which has commingled with the wine as a part of the covenant communion ceremony of remembrance of flesh and blood entering into them a little at a time. Prince Liam receives the last portion of His joyous meal of eternity.

Once everyone has eaten and been satisfied, I notice that the cups are still full and announce, "Puppco, come forward. From this time forth you will be the Eucharistic Minister until an assigned priest comes to your community. These elements of bread and wine shall remain fresh and never run out until that time." He places the small cup and filled container on the ground at the foot of the altar with a final word, "They are to be distributed at morn everyday and I leave it to you to appoint successors to aid you in this task."

"How is all of this possible?"

"There are rules of man which make laws by what is seen inside his mind, but then there are the rules of nature in creation, pointing to the Creator's hand as all is possible within the laws of God."

Puppco bows his head and raises it with the answer, "Understood."

Prince Liam gestures with his arm to Ashley and asks, "Are you ready for travel?"

I answer, "Quite."

Drawing his sword, he takes about ten paces and starts to carve out a trail through some overgrown thickets. Ashley walks behind him and I sense by the Spirit which rests upon the throne of my heart that the Lord is walking with us all. We soon break into some open woods and Liam sheaths his sword. Then taking Ashley by the hand, they begin a romantic walk in the woods. The sunlight glistens through the trees and I am reminded of my romance of The Great One who ignites my soul with a flame of His own as a true soulmate embraces from within. After walking in the joy of the Lord for about an hour in fellowship with His wooded splendors, Prince Liam draws his sword and begins hacking away at some more thickets which turn to underbrush.

Bursting out from the cover of forest, we find ourselves on an open riverbank. About a mile down river, I can see the mist rising from the waterfall. Looking the other way, Prince Liam motions with his hand to walk up river. This is when I see the *Hope it Floats* from off in the distance, which we start walking towards.

The sun rises to an eleven o'clock high and if not for the cool of the water, I know it would be much hotter.

We walk along the riverbank at a quarter pace and the rocks by the water gradually become smaller until there is beach sand. Taking my eyes from The Great One, I start to get waves of thoughts about not having my long knife or pack. Then while losing my sense of presence of being, my mind drifts as though I'm being carried by the waves of the river. "Bam!" My face hits the sand as I have tripped over my own steps and fallen from not watching where I was going.

Prince Liam hears my fall and turns around. As he places his hand under my arm, he asks, "Are you okay?" I nod and he helps me to my feet.

Ashley then asks, "Just before you fell, what had your vision?"

"I was wondering about my long knife and provisions in my pack that was left behind. Oh! If I had only known we were not going back for them, I would have at least taken my knife."

The prince further questions, "What just happened in the gnome village back there, Marcus? Did The Great One not perform a Eucharistic miracle, Priest?"

"Forgive my lack of faith as I know I have been a poor example before you both. Though even now, I remember that the Lord shall provide. Great One, I have grieved my loss of provision and forgotten that You are the One who provides. Let us be off again to the *Hope it Floats*."

I pick up the pace and now walk in the Lord's confidence with a watchful boldness to my step. As we approach the ship, Skip sees us and rings the ship's bell to encourage us on and alert the others. While we look at the boat and the welcoming faces with waves, all at once I hear the whining of horses. We all stop and turn our heads to see Claire and Ezmarelda on Ashley's gray horse, leading Liam's black with my pack, long Knife which sticks slightly out, and other provisions.

Shaking my head, I grin and say, "You two coming to see us off is a beautiful sight."

Claire responds, "I took a step of faith concerning what was revealed to a vision of Ezmarelda's, but I'm glad I did, for it warms my heart to see you all again." Her sister sits behind her with a wide smile and nods her head.

All at once, we hear the splash of the longboat hitting the water. Then turning our heads, Oxer is seen at the oars with Captain Cantik at the bow as they get gradually closer.

Dismounting from the horse, the two lead them onto the beach with supply and all. Next, everything happened so suddenly. The eyes of Cantik look up as he turns to meet Claire's eyes. He looks back. After the pulling of the longboat ashore slows to a pause and tipping his cap, the captain introduces himself,

"My name be Cantik and who would you be, fair lady?"

Clair answers with a blush, "Mine is Claire."

"Perhaps you would like to go for a sail on my boat, the *Hope it Floats*?"

"What a name for a ship."

"It might seem a bit odd of a name, but it always gets me where I am going."

"It sounds like something I'd like to do, but I really would like to get to know its captain a little better before I get on his ship."

"Oxer, prepare the water barrels and fetch some fresh water with the cart. Then get the long-boat loaded while the fair lady Claire and I take in some air on the beach. I am sure that the others will give you a hand."

"Aye, captain."

Prince Liam approaches Cantik and Claire who are walking side by side. "I see you two have met…"

"…And are still meeting. Oxer will be loading the longboat while lady Claire and I go for a walk. He will take any instruction you might have."

"What I have to say can wait 'til we're on the ship. Carry on."

"We won't be long, Prince Liam."

Cantik smiles and the two proceed to walk the beach. Ashley and I advance towards the longboat where Ezmarelda steadies the horses while Oxer begins unpacking them.

"Let me give you a hand, Oxer," says the prince. He reaches up, unties my pack, and hands it to me. I place it in the longboat. The second mate goes to uncinch the saddle from the horse but Liam stops him, "No, Oxer. Just the bags. The saddles need to remain on the horses for them to know to find their own way home."

I ask, "What do you mean? Aren't we going back to the monastery?"

"On our way here, the Great One impressed it upon my mind for us to go back with you to your seaport of Sedwick."

"Well, okay."

I ask a second time, "Why are we going to Sedwick?"

"Don't know yet. You look disappointed, Marcus."

"It's because I thought I was going to see Sono again."

"They'll be other times."

"I guess you're right."

The last of the church bride is receiving the meal of eternal life from the bridegroom's hand at the marriage supper of The Lamb's table. Then everyone returns to their place. "This mass has ended. Go in peace," is heard by the Monsignor.

Those who have decided to leave old winnies field bid their farewells to Bashna who is joyous over having his wife, Bella, by his side again. Sono walks next to the Monsignor who rides behind Edward on his horse. Everyone begins to fall in line with their push carts from the village at winnies field. They have taken on plenty of water as the desert crossing awaits after a bit of travel through the Great Forest up ahead.

Prince Liam helps the second mate at the rear of the water barrel wagon, which seems to roll down the beach towards the longboat on its own.

Oxer calls out, "Quick! Slow the wagon with a counter pull from the rear or we'll ram the longboat if we come in too quickly."

The prince digs in the sand with his boot heels and leans back as he straddles forward with the wagon. "Just when I thought it was going to get easy."

Upon arrival at the longboat, Oxer starts to load the water barrels by rolling them up a plank while Liam goes over to the horses and starts them on their swim across the river before their long journey home.

Captain Cantik sees the horses in the water and realizes it is time to head back to the longboat. When they arrive, Prince Liam inquires, "Well, what have you two been talking about?"

The Captain responds, "How mature we've become since our youth as we both have obligations to put off before getting to know each other. When I come back and visit again, it will be a more appropriate time." Cantik turns and looks Claire in the eyes and says while raising her hand to where it meets his lips with a kiss, "Until we meet again."

Claire blushes, takes back her hand, and holds it up to her heart while looking on as her words slowly leave her lips, "I will wait for the timing of The Great One on this."

"I am just going across the river, Lady Claire."

"We need to go to Sedwick, captain," says Prince Liam.

"Then why did you start the horses to swim across?"

"They will find their own way home."

Ashley looks on and smiles at Claire.

Captain Cantik agrees, "Well, I guess it will be in the beauty of The Great One's timing as now I will have to wait, too."

Ashley suggests, "A love which knows how to wait is a love that is true. For being willing to wait, clarity comes and God rewards. Now, I want you to know that you shall be a member of our lineage if you pursue Claire as she is my mother. So, you better beware as I can guarantee that The Great One will be watching you by my personal prayers."

"I believe love to be priceless. Although, now that you mention it, I do see a resemblance. So, how is it that your mother lives in Dagog and where is your father?"

"He is dead. Murdered by a nephilim."

"How did all this come about… and why do you need to go to Sedwick, Prince Liam?"

"I know not why yet as The Great One has not revealed it to me."

Ashley interjects, "You are right in what you said, Captain, true love is priceless. I will tell you of our story after we set sail on the *Hope it Floats* as it will tell a further glory of what The Great One can do."

"Then what are we waiting for? Let us get underway."

Claire and Ezmarelda wave as Captain Cantik and the second mate shove off. With Oxer at the oars, they rapidly advance towards the ship.

Breaking from the Great Forest, all bid their final farewells to those who have tagged along. Sono, who is among them, stands aside and watches as Edward and the Monsignor lead everyone onward. As they do so, Romp, the first to have been changed back from being a dust winnie and chosen leader when the truth was tested, rides alongside Prince Edward's horse and says, "Lively bunch of little ones those dwarfs are."

"They're just like that because they've newly been set free from an enchantment," says the Monsignor.

"What enchantment?"

"Why don't you tell him, Monsignor? I need to keep my bearing while we cross the desert."

"Well, Romp, what I am about to tell you shall be a help in understanding many points of view while in leadership. To start off, all minds are affected spiritually behind mere physical appearances, which is a reason for many infirmities and that of mind."

"Having been a sand creature of dust, believe you me, I understand that what has our focus from thoughts beneath words behind actions can determine a light of life or death of darkness situation."

"Then you know how evil can be pretty crafty in the way it seduces a mind. For behind what might seem innocent may seduce an untrained mind away from having a full relationship with the love of God."

"I know of what you speak, Monsignor. For if we were without this knowledge, we could have been provoked into a war against each other back at the village early on. I recognize that there will be many tests to see if our faith be true or not as we've all been trained from the *Book of Life* to discern any spirits that might hide in the darkness of a dragon night."

"Then the Lord will bless you in the movement of His timing, Romp, as He will always do."

"I am grateful for our Lord's timing of our trip and fully acknowledge His hand in it. I have a feeling that we shall pass any test. For in knowing each other well, we shall be kept tried and true, which will guard our steps to stand throughout any land and keep us from the entrance of hell."

"Romp, I am sure before all is said and done that you of all will know more of God's mercy for the sake of everyone."

"All my boasting is in the Lord. For this is the way our government works. So, how can anything go wrong?"

"We shall see."

"Everyone here has already passed the test as the nature of this trip is due to our faithfulness."

"A heated dispute with a threat of war. Really?"

"Surely you jest. Remember there was no war."

"Perhaps you're right, as sometimes I must confess that my tongue can be rather quick."

Romp then adds, "So, let me hear your story for perhaps in all humility, there is something more I need to learn, especially when an enchantment is concerned."

Sailing quickly up the Dailey River, we hit the currents fast and hard with the sounding pole on the ready at the bow in Oxer's hands. We pass the reef at the river's mouth and catch the tide of the ocean, which takes us off the coast. The skies are clear and as nightfall comes after eve, Captain Cantik hands the wheel over to skip while he makes his way to the cabin. Upon entry, he joins us at the table sitting across from Ashley and Liam and next to me at his right hand side.

"If I am not interrupting anything, I'm finally ready to hear about what your mother spoke to you about her testimony to the glory of Jesus, our Great One and King."

Ashley clears her throat, tightly holding Liam's hand. When she relaxes her grip, she is ready to begin. "I am going to tell you the facts as I've heard them from my mother when she came to visit me at the castle.

Originally, we were all from the province of Bilatz. Claire was discovered with child and that child was me. My father's name was Eugene and he had two brother's, one of which was married to my aunt Nilda who unfortunately was not able to get pregnant. One of my uncles remained behind to look after things in Bilatz and came to look for us much later on. My father came along with my other uncle in search of an angel in the mountains of Dagog to ask favor. They wanted to have a son so that Nilda could be with child, too.

My other aunts came along because they had never been to the mountains and were curious to see what an angel looked like. It seems on their search while journeying through the mountains of Dagog that they were attacked by the sons of fallen angels called nephilim. These were giants, five of them in all, which took them by surprise. I heard that they lay in wait in the clefs of the rocks near to where the caverns of their home now be.

A battle ensued where Eugene and his brother fought hard as they managed to draw their swords. They were surrounded with no hope of escape but were quick in standing back to back and were able to keep them away as the first one fell when my father cut off his leg while shouting, "Stay focused!" to his brother. The second giant fell with a jab to his groin, again by my father who was quick to withdraw his sword. Then ducking a sword which wooshed over his head, he stabbed the third in his side through his armor. This is when he lost his sword as it could not be withdrawn. So, he took out his knife and threw it in the eye of the fourth who came charging, killing him instantly with its force. His brother went down and before the fifth could retrieve his sword, my father bit his arm 'til it seemed like he could do no more harm. For when my father went for its throat, he was slain by the giant, cutting him through."

"Your father was a brave man."

"Thank you, captain."

"He was fierce…"

"…Yes, although unfortunately, all the giants did not die right away 'til their infections set in much later. Though it was customary to eat the dead of those who died in battle to gain their strength and live after grinding their bones. The one who was missing a leg was bleeding so bad that when he went to eat father raw, he choked on one of his ribs and died on the spot.

They thought my father's spirit was too strong afterwards and buried the rest of his body out of respect instead. His brother's body was left on the staff of a great spear to deter anyone from passing higher into the mountains as they were wounded and needed time to heal."

"How is it that they kept your mother and aunts alive?"

In a way, you might say that I saved them. For my mother was showing with me and as they practiced the ritual of spells, one of which was if a mother gave birth and they ate her baby while it breathed its first, they would gain the spirit of its life and live.

My mother, Claire, told them that she would only offer me, without killing me first, if they let her and all her sisters live. Horrible and unspeakable things were done to them that they would learn black crafts for the giant's personal gain and while they prepared, because my mother was with child, she was able to obtain the power of more demons. While they were at the giant's lair, the remaining nephilim died off one at a time from being infected by their wounds wrought of my father."

"How is it that you're still here?"

"My remaining uncle came looking for us when we did not return. The remaining giant hid all of his weapons, keeping them out of sight for fear of my mother and aunts using them upon him while he slept, all except a razor sharp knife of sacrifice, which he kept under a great polished rock that he rested his head on while he slept. This is how my remaining uncle killed him. While he slept within the cave, my father's remaining brother stood in watch. He staked us out and as the nephilim slept, he entered the caves and did him in while he slept.

They wouldn't leave the cavern area after all was done, so my uncle stayed to care for them. Understand that after all the torture they went through from all they knew, they learned to hate as their resentments grew."

"Is your uncle yet alive? I would like to meet him."

"You already have as he travels with Prince Edward even now."

Captain Cantik's jaw drops down as he mouths out the words, "The Monsignor is your uncle?"

"Yes. God made him faithful with little before over much."

"Remarkable!"

Beneath stars under a dark sky of desert, "Remarkable story of enchantment!" says Romp while they yet travel in the cool of night upon the sands. "Now I know what you meant by saying that I would learn of how merciful our Great One is for the sake of everyone."

Prince Edward holds up his hand, "Woe!" Stopping his horse, he examines the night sky. The hundred men and their families stop while Edward gets his bearings.

Romp inquires of the Monsignor, "Are we lost?"

"Believe you me. Prince Edward knows his stars…" The Monsignor taps Edward on the shoulder and points slightly to the right.

"Thank you, Monsignor."

"…Almost as well as I."

The moon travels with Prince Edward throughout the night and into the first light of the morn at twilight. As the sun peeks out over the familiar Tall Hills, the mountains of Zantee can be seen coming into view off in the distance because of the clarity of day. Soon after, buckets from those who travel with the caravan hit the waters of the seeing pools in the woods.

"It won't be long now, Romp, as there is only one more place to stop for water after here." He dismounts his horse along with the Monsignor and Edward and they begin to stretch their legs.

"We could settle here. This is a rather pleasant place," says Romp.

"Others have tried to settle here, but the seeing pools of the land itself do not allow it. As this is a sacred place, an unspoiled place of earth and must remain so for others or the balance of dreams and visions of all would be disrupted. You can stay for a short season, but more than that, the pools them-selves would cry out for rains and the area would become flooded 'til you could not remain. This is why those who come looking for answers here often get messages from its pools."

"I will respect what you say, Monsignor."

Prince Edward mounts his horse and makes a proclamation, "Gather yourselves, everyone. We're moving out!" He extends his hand and helps the Monsignor on his horse from behind his. The people fall in line as Romp mounts his horse and soon we are on the road again."

Prince Edward and the Monsignor are enjoying a peaceful ride while taking in the scenery when Romp comes up to them and says, "Perhaps one of you would have a lesson for me as I am always eager to learn something new. For I have forsaken all to follow after The Great One."

"Do you really want to learn?" asks the prince.

"What do you mean?"

"Are you sure you do not know everything already having forsaken all while walking with your Master and Friend?"

"Has The Great One as Christ carried you here or did you come on your own accord, believing it was in His name?"

"Please explain further because I am confused."

The Monsignor explains,"I see that you are ready for a lesson now as you are in need of one."

Prince Edward enters the mountain pass of Zantee as all leave the Tall Hills right in line right behind them.

"What I wish to know is, did you leave darkness on your own to enter the Spirit of light without any change of your location, other than to do everything as unto the Lord to embrace eternal life?" asks the Monsignor.

"Doth the *Book of Life* not say, "That no one who forsakes family, children or mother and father shall receive back much more than what they have left behind?"

"But doth that not mean to change your physical location or be sharpened to shine brighter where you abide until someone sees the reflection of His light in you, and then acknowledge that all of you has been made brand new?"

"Now I understand the parable, 'A light is not to be hidden under a basket, but to be placed on a lampstand,' as a lampstand doth not move!" shouts Romp.

"I believe he understands, Monsignor."

"The verse, 'I am the vine and you are the branches and apart from me you can do nothing unless you abide in me,' ties in here as well," says the Monsignor.

Soon after exiting the mountain pass, over to our left, we come into the view of villagers looking on.

They watch as all draw near to the village. We appear, coming out of the dust kicked up by the wind. Finally, they all come to a stop.

Trevor makes a bold statement to Prince Edward, "Why did you bring them here without first notifying us?"

"For passage to Sedwick. Please accept my apology for my lack of sight, Trevor."

"Sedwick is still our town!"

"No one lives there now and they could bring it back to life again."

"Not under my authority as its mayor."

" I will have council with the Monsignor and Romp, who is the leader of this band of men and their families. If you'd be kind enough to wait here after we three talk and are in agreement as one voice, then we shall be heard."

"Fair enough."

They ride off a hundred yards with the wind at their backs.

Romp speaks first, "I say we can take them rather easily."

The Monsignor speaks next, "Is this the kind of example you want to set for your children? Take what you want when you want it. This doth not sound like the mercy you spoke of earlier to me."

"Then what would you propose, Monsignor?"

"If the seaport of Sedwick was taken by wiping out the villagers here, righteous blood would cry out and you would have no peace of mind at the seaport after a season. Then there are your children to consider as violence begets violence."

Romp punches his hand with his fist, "You're right! What do you say, Prince Edward?"

"I say show him the map with Captain Cantik's mark…"

"…and what if he refuses to recognize it?" asks the Monsignor.

"Then we would be justified in wiping them out," says Romp.

"As The Great One has shown us mercy, we are to be merciful, too. Remember, He has laid down His life for us to this end. He loves all of us."

The two look to the Monsignor at the same time and ask, "What would you suggest?"

"Sedwick is probably a town that he helped to build up from scratch and put a lot of sweat into doing it. He has cultivated this village at Ostrog well and has probably put even more care into the seaport. Yet, now he has a priest who is in league with us. They know us to be brothers, so we should treat them as such.

At this point, Sedwick is probably more of a sentiment to him emotionally than having any physical property. First, we should pray with him 'til there is peace between us all. Second, we should offer him a house of honor that would be kept for him in town, which he could visit anytime he wants as a part of a family of brotherhood. Third, we shall remind him that the town would be maintained and kept in working order. Fourth, we shall present him with the note with Cantik's mark. Then we shall see if he has counter terms, such as supporting him with a defense if he has a just cause, which would be a fifth term. Then if need be, we can suggest to him if he remains undecided, collecting a town tax that he would receive as a percentage.

There are so many ways to have a peaceful resolution. We must remain civil and temperate or evil spirits would again be invited to possess us to a point of annihilation and have their way with our souls. This is why we must keep our eyes on The Great One who is the giver of life. Peace must be maintained at all costs. For when we can reason together, peace shall keep us in soundness of mind to remain alive and sane.

While the terms are about to be presented, a commotion is heard approaching 'til Prince Liam appears, "Was not sure of what to do when we got to Sedwick last night 'til I had a season of prayer. What's been happening as of late?"

"As usual, you are a sight for sore eyes, brother."

"You're looking pretty good to me too, Edward."

Upon seeing Prince Liam, Trevor asks if he would reside over the terms as they are presented.

"What do you say, Edward?"

"It's a good idea as the terms are fair."

"Alright, Trevor. I will sit among everyone and hear the terms and see if they really are fair or not."

"Thank you, Prince Liam."

"No thanks to me. How about we pray and start out by thanking the Great One together?"

# Back at the Kingdom

Two horses, black and gray, make their appearance with no riders at Calington Castle.

Once seen by the guard at the gate, they are taken into the castle.

Upon hearing news of the horses without riders from a messenger, King Henry calls out from his throne, "Prepare my horse, gather the guard, and send for the healer."

The queen is seen praying from her throne as King Henry pauses momentarily by the keeper of the gate and says, "Have word sent to Luis and Andrea to pray for the royal family and all our safe returns." He rides out of the gate with the healer by his side, along with some of his trusted guards who lead Prince Liam and Ashley's horses from behind.

The response, "Yes, your majesty!" is heard.

Making for the road, a discussion ensues between the healer and the king.

"Your majesty, I can see how upset you are. Before we ride hard, remember that all things happen in The Great One's timing and by Him, everyone has an exit to leave here alive rather than dead inside. So, plan for the worst in your heart and keep your hope by prayer as you must not lose touch with your feelings and go numb inside. For being in this world and not of it, we receive the completion of a new covenant life to its fullest."

"As usual, your counsel is most accurate, my friend."

After a pause, one of the guards inquires, "Where to, your majesty?"

"We last had word of them heading for the monastery. Let us ride there first and The Lord shall direct us from there."

Trevor ponders for a moment, "The terms seem fair… What say you, Prince Liam, as one who raises the dead can bring light to any situation?"

I feel a tribute should be collected from a percentage of taxes for ten years in addition to the other terms. Then you shall be compensated for the work you have put into your town."

"I trust your words, Prince Liam," says Trevor. "They are agreeable to me."

"Well, what do you say, Romp?" inquires the Monsignor.

"Let me ride among the men and see if they are in agreement. We shall put it to a vote. Although in all fairness, I should tell you that I do not like making an agreement without having first seen the town. I am sure that there will be others that feel the same way as I do. Perhaps after we have seen this town… we can then make a better determination."

"Prince Liam, what do you say?" asks Trevor.

"Have you quill and parchment among you?"

"Why, yes."

"The Monsignor will draw up these terms as follows… Romp, you and your men will be given thirty days to settle in the town. Those of you who do not like it can leave and settle elsewhere with no obligation beforehand."

"Well done, brother."

"God is good and you shall be more than satisfied as I have seen the town, Romp."

"By your word, this term will be added, Prince Liam. I am now in agreement and will tell the men. Then putting it to a vote, an answer will be determined," says Romp.

"Draw up the paper, Monsignor. For I am in agreement, too," says Trevor.


King Henry reaches a sign that says, "This way to the valley of the dragon."

The healer suggests, "If the prince and the others should return this way, we will miss them. We should split up and meet back on the main road. This way, we'll cover more ground."

King Henry takes a strong stand, "I need to pray."

"Your majesty, why doth the freedom of your peace with The Great One seem shakened?"

"This is why I need to pray… Alright, what do you see that I do not?"

"If prayer be forced and regimented, there is no enjoyment with whom you speak. So, how can I be in agreement with this thread, which is unlike any other in the full garment of our relationship?"

"You are right. All of the water is turbulent that surrounds my mind as I am not at peace. Pray for me as I have lost my way to finding our Maker's hand who rules over all the heaven and spirits of earth."

The healer looks to the king and says, "Remove thy crown in the name of The Great One and be at peace."

"I was surviving in self-reliance because I had forgotten to rely on God. Thank you for reminding me, old friend."

King Henry smiles and asks for two volunteers to go through *The Valley of the Dragon* and says, "Meet me on the other side on the main road."

There is apprehension on the part of his men. So, Henry encourages, "If I were younger and a little more durable, I would have not even hesitated to go through this pass. For I know that in facing my fears, the reward of a deeper love is always near. I asked for two volunteers as the reward of a deeper love is that it casts away all fears. You know where two or more are gathered in His name, He is in our midst. The Great One is a rewarder of those who diligently seek Him and is greater than any foul dragon spirits of this created world by the craft of His own hand. Now, who of you will step forward and be blessed by God this day?

The healer steps down and hands Henry the reins to his horse after saying, "I can always use another blessing."

"I volunteer!" says one of the guards." As he steps forward, King Henry extends his hand with a skin filled with water and suggests with a kind gesture, "Take this water, you two. It is my extra skin. I'm giving you this cause I trust to see you soon."

The healer takes it in hand and says. "See you on the other side, old friend."

"Guard, what is your name?"

"Wilfred, your majesty."

"Well, Wilfred, you shall dine with our family when we get back."

"Thank you, sir!"

The healer and Wilfred start for the valley while King Henry and the others continue along the main road.

Romp stands before Trevor on his return after the votes have been tallied. We wait together with concern, he then gives his awaited answer, "All the men agree to the terms."

"Praise be to The Great One and Prince Liam for being used to speak so wisely. Hooray!"

Trevor instructs Romp to alert the others that they will be moving out, "Have them line up at the well, this way they can fill their buckets and skins with a fresh water supply before they journey to Sedwick."

Prince Edward looks to his brother Liam, Ashley is by his side. "Looks like we are in for a bit of a walk back to the Castle, Liam.

"Have faith. I am sure The Great One will provide us with a little thing like transportation unless He wants us to walk."

Before long, Romp returns. All are lined up for water at the well.

Trevor makes the comment, "That's quite a band of men you have among you. How did such a diverse lot come together? So many of your men appear to be from different provinces.

"Well, it is a bit of a long story."

Trevor looks back towards the well, "It looks like I have some time to listen."

"Oh! Where are my manners? Thank you for letting us have water to refresh ourselves."

Trevor extends his hand, "Your welcome, brother. after all, doth everyone not have a story to tell?"

"Is this an invitation to spend the night?"

"Why not? There is nothing like a good story."

Standing on the road are the healer and Wilfred. King Henry and the other guards approach. He inquires of his friend, "Well, what happened in the valley?"

The healer then gives report, "There is really nothing to speak of within the valley. Though at the end of the valley, there was an altar set as a mark of someone meeting The Great One. This was further confirmed by a group of villagers who had met a young hooded priest about the time Prince Liam went missing. It was during your illness from the spell of your thirst for strong wine. If there was a dragon in that valley, Prince Liam must have defeated it by the Great One's own hand. This would be the only explanation for the altar."

"Sounds like we should have that sign taken down."

"Perhaps, *Prince Liam's Pass* would be an appropriate name as he has done so much for our kingdom by seeking the truth."

King Henry notices the guard standing with a smile on his face next to the healer and asks, "Have you anything to report, Wilfred?"

"Our healer is in love."

The healer blushes and is bashful in his words, "I was going to tell you about a most noble queen named Samantha and her daughter, Princess Danielle, who were given their positions by standing up against a witch when continuing our ride."

The King commands, "Bring them their horses and let us be on our way as I have to hear of this. After all, the healer did say he could always use another blessing before entering *Prince Liam's Pass*."


Marcus suggests to the Monsignor, "It looks like our journey has ended as what started out as my vision has been fully revealed. When should we head back to the monastery?"

"I am praying for a season of quality time with my daughter before we head back."

"Marcus calls out, "Ashley, your uncle would like a word with you."

"What is it, uncle?"

The Monsignor motions with his hand for her to come over and says to Marcus, "Thank you."

On arrival, Ashley asks, "What is it, uncle?"

"I have grown in wisdom on how to relate to you better. Yet, time is so short and there is much to teach in the way of giving you a heritage of wealth to pass down to future generations. Your obligations to the kingdom have now become distractions as to what is really important, a full relationship with our God who lives forever. Please don't just settle for the things you can grasp in your hand as The Spirit of The Great One is richer still. He has a wealth that lasts for an eternity."

"You are right, uncle. Thank you for this awakening. Do you have any strategy on how to do battle against this dragon that, while unaware, I have taken into my hands?"

"Pray 'til your light shines with Him upon your face. For when other people inquire about what you possess and not what possesses you, you can again share the way of what will cause them to be eternally alive inside forever."

"I will do this as by your word, The Great Ones flame has been lit in my heart again."

"Why not come and stay at the Monastery with me for a season 'til you fully be ignited again?"

"My husband needs me."

"Yet is the Lord not a husband to all who have become one with Him in baptism? Come study The Great One again and after a season of having distractions removed, everyone you know will be the better for it."

"This is something I need to discuss with Liam as I am now no longer completely my own."

"I am aware of this. Just know that I love you no matter what is decided. Although, I suggest you ask him now as I will tarry for your answer. This way if he says yes, you can return with me."

"I understand and will ask him now." Taking leave of her uncle, she approaches Liam.

Edward is talking as she draws near, "I suggest we take up Trevor on his offer to stay the night as we have to rest up for our long journey's home."

Ashley comes up to them while they speak and interjects, "Speaking of journeys, I need a vacation to retreat back into the Lord's kingdom. For the torch of my heart has been going dim as of late and needs to ignite again."

While Ashley is talking to her husband and Edward about the monastery, Marcus comments to the Monsignor from a distance, "Do you believe that we'll have company on our return trip?"

"God only knows."

All at once, a guard can be heard calling out, "Make way for his excellency, King Henry of Calington Castle." The entourage of push carts and travelers make way for the royal king and his guards with the healer by his side.

On seeing this, Prince Liam cries out, "Father, we're over here!"

Riding up to Liam, King Henry sighs with relief, "I should have known that you were in the midst of all this."

"What has brought you all the way out here, father?"

"Guards!" Hoof beats are heard on the ground.

Liam looks over, "Mine and Ashley's horses! This is just what we need on our ride to the monastery."

"The monastery? I thought you were coming back to the castle."

"Father, Ashley has given me a marvelous idea which you are welcome to join us on, I only ask that you hear her first before you decide?"

"Very well. What is it, daughter?"

Marcus turns to the Monsignor and says, "If your niece is as persuasive as you are, it looks like we'll be getting a ride back to the monastery. After All, who's to say that the purpose of this whole trip was for everyone to return to the kingdom and know The Great One more?"

"Like I told you before, God only knows."

# Epilogue
## A Lesson at the Monastery

A crowd sits in the courtyard of the monastery in the large open area just beyond the floral garden near the front. It is determined that everyone who sits is seated in a humble place of royalty as being servants to all, they are priests.

The Monsignor speaks a message that is near and dear, especially since King Henry and most of the royal family are there. His voice is loud and clear, "When you want to do something that is good, beware of any voices that say you should. If something is not genuine, a part of who you are, you go missing in the dark. Then who is really sitting on the throne of your heart in the midst of your wanting to do something right? Remember now that God wants us to be *beings* that are at rest as He is at peace within the midst of all uneasiness. Now Marcus has a few words to share on this matter, as well."

"I started my first trip with Bartholomew and always raced ahead to do something for the Great One's kingdom of peace. Yet, I never knew that He was not on the throne of my heart, for restlessness is never His home. Finally, when I slowed my pace, things started to come into view. I saw that by the abruptness of my pace, I had been mutilating myself with anxious holes which I, myself, tore into the fibers of my being. I had surrendered to an anxiety of abuse which I called life, but I was really dying inside. For demons know verses from the *Book of Life*, too. Trembling compulsively in minds, disturbing flesh which dies in the dimness of pride. Blindly, all who are unknowing pass on and get punished here. Yes, at the beginning of our journey, I dwelt uncomfortably in heart and mind 'til slowing down to see how I became frozen, which ignited me into going against the friction of my pace. Then like a rock against waves of an ocean, I started to stand in the stillness of The Great One's presence who gave me peace for perspective while in the dark. It was then by the light of His glory that I started to understand, which broke the waves of commotion 'til all became calm.

The more I slowed my mind, the more the stillness of God's presence filled me. When crafted by His hand of Spirit, the gift of His peace was contained within my soul as I had yielded to the kingdom of eternal life. Then the question came to mind, 'Do I want to be at peace and enjoy being alive or be distracted from who is giving me life? I must not take the hand of foreign spirits, which abuse and confuse through a force that distracts many from love.'

The blood of Christ brings peace because it is incorruptibly complete as it yields to the peace of His kingdom of *being*. For what has true royal worth belongs only to peace. The blood of His word flows through me with life in the new covenant offering by His Spirit as one seamless garment for the body of The Great One. This is how He functions through us in His timing.

My mind is being renewed in the glory of His kingdom from the transformation of transfusion by His resurrecting blood which springs up and sings unto eternal life. Pray for the spirits of this world to die down so that seed can be planted to rightly know the truth as The Great One's word is in a state of being alive from a root of New Covenant blood, allowing us to forever remain in heaven."

Bartholomew rises and leans on his walking stick. Suddenly, becoming spirited, he leaps with joy and says, "The time for small doses of heaven is coming to an end, for to be absent from the body is to be present with the Lord! So, no longer fear the great dragon of earth which had us hooked, dragging us on lines to distract with self will, which at one time took us away from the hand of God as His peace now has a presence to bring light to any situation. He is here and we are there with Him when we are in the freedom of the kingdom of eternal life. For while in the present moment of His love, we are in this world but no longer of it. We stand in the authority of a light in a present darkness at the open door in the midst of all time. By His presence, we can come to the table and drink to sustain eternal life. So, walk in the light in the essence of God without being moved when the spirits call and you shall be filled with a life that maintains all sight with the honor of The Great One's light."

I watch as a sense of awe falls on everyone from the words of the ripe fruit just spoken by His light and they are life. Blessed are those who thirst for this path as they will always be satisfied by doing what is right.

Meanwhile, on the trail to the seaport, there are whispering thoughts on the air that ride concealed within the dark, *"You don't have to present the paper with Trevor, Prince Liam, and the Monsignor's marks. No taxes need be paid this way. Why, Captain Cantik would never have to know. How would he find out?"* Romp hears these voices as his own within his ears as they attempt to divide his mind of light while he leads. He then begins to reason while he wrestles within, *"What if God is not truth itself as is light not really night when most people see without seeing anyway?"* More thoughts come to trouble Romp while on the trail cut out earlier by myself when traveling with the Monsignor and Sono.

In the midst of the battle, the conviction of The Great One falls on him, *"You would be wise to do right as Cantik's mark is there as well. He shall anticipate his paper as a sign before officially accepting you into town."*

"Lord, how am I the leader of these others when I cannot even lead myself? Have mercy on us all."

Captain Cantik talks with his crew as all leave the boat at the dock, "Come on, gents, let's take in the silence of the town that has been talking to us all of these years. It is going to live again, although all the new people who are coming in may speak another silence to us 'til we get to know them.

Skip, you have a bright mind. I want to set you over the coin of what comes into the town treasury. Oxer, you will be in charge of collecting the taxes. We shall have coin set aside for Trevor as it is only right, seeing how he helped build this town."

Looking back at the boat docked at the seaport from up on the hill, they all notice how distant it has become. Oxer comments, "Ya mean we are not gonna sail anymore?"

"It will be a little hard in the beginning 'til we learn who we can trust responsibly, but after others are set to help out, I believe we'll have time for short trips."

Skip asks, "Are you sure this is what you want, captain?"

"They are going to have leaders, Skip. Besides, Prince Liam never would have asked this of us unless he knew all would work out alright."

"What happens if we don't get along?"

"Have a little faith, Skip, and remember that we are doing this as unto The Great One who has said, "Anyone who gives a cup of water in my name shall not lose their reward. I believe only good is going to come out of this. So, let us focus on loving The Great One so that we may receive a king's reward."

Skip responds, "I believe that we'll sail again."

"Come, it may soon be time to greet our new guests."

"How can you tell?" asks Oxer.

Skip responds, "Can't you smell them on the breeze?" He motions with his hand, "After you, captain."

"Aye-aye."

Rounding the turn at the top of the hill where the Monsignor, Sono, and I had first come into town long ago, they see the men from Old Winnies field with tears of joy being led by someone who looks to be in charge. Watching Captain Cantik and his men slowly approach, the leader of the villagers turns to them and excuses himself before he starts to take steps towards the others down the street as a tumbleweed blows across their path.

Meeting in the middle of town, Cantik steps away from his men and extends his hand as they meet eye to eye with a pause. Their leader extends his hand as well and says, "My name is Romp, and thank you for opening your town to us."

Captain Cantik takes his hand and responds while they shake, "We meet at last."

**-The end is only the beginning-**

# About the Author

R. A. Feller is an internationally acclaimed award winning poet who has taken on the challenge to truly find out what it means to be alive inside.

Find out what he has found on his over 40 years of journeying with pen in hand to find out the meaning in his almost 64 years of life.

Look for R. A. Feller's new book coming soon: "The Tree of Life"